LASSITER: BLOOD RIVER

Lassiter likes money, women and booze — in that order, and he'll kill, steal and cheat to get them. He has the morals of a jack rabbit, the ethics of a landgrabber and the conscience of a cold-blooded gunslick. He takes what he wants, when he wants, and to hell with everyone else.

JACK SLADE

LASSITER BLOOD RIVER

Complete and Unabridged

LINFORD
Leicester

First published in Great Britain in 1974 by
Belmont Tower Books
New York

First Linford Edition
published March 1991

British Library CIP Data

Slade, Jack, *b. 1903–*
    Blood river.—Large print ed.—
Linford western library
Rn: Willis Todhunter Ballard I. Title
813.54 [F]

ISBN 0–7089–6968–2

Published by
F. A. Thorpe (Publishing) Ltd.
Anstey, Leicestershire

Set by Words & Graphics Ltd.
Anstey, Leicestershire
Printed and bound in Great Britain by
T. J. Press (Padstow) Ltd., Padstow, Cornwall

1

THE river boat *Aurora* shivered constantly, battered by the wild current that poured down from the Idaho wilderness, and in the night a woman whimpered in sudden terror. She was aft on the port side, the side away from the bank where the boat was tethered — improbably clad only in a thin nightgown with a long skirt, with light from stars and a crescent moon explicitly silhouetting her statuesque figure. A man gripping her hard, with profane grated whispers, tore at the gown, ripping it almost from her.

"You two-faced bitch!" he said. "You've double-crossed me for the last time!"

She whimpered again, eyes wide in terror.

Lassiter stepped from his shoebox of a stateroom he had taken rather than join the forward crowd that was riding the *Aurora*'s lower deck to the new gold diggings up-river in the Blue Horns.

Pale marbled flesh was revealed as the nightgown was all but stripped away, suavely rounded firmness of a bosom that might have graced Athena, the Queen Goddess — and beauty of features to match, with swirl of hair that was chestnut-brown in color, something Lassiter had observed when she came aboard the *Aurora* at sunset.

Now, forced back against the cabin deck railing as though her attacker meant to shove her into the racing flood of Kiskadee River, she struggled turgidly as he mauled her with a fist. "You're for the fish and the buzzards, sweetheart," he said venomously. "It's what you've bought with your cheating . . ."

Lassiter went at the man, left hand out to grip a shoulder as teak-hard as the boat rail itself. No matter, however; the toughest of hard-cases had points of vulnerability, and he now attacked one, with whip of his Colt .44 from where it was thrust under his belt.

He did not squeeze trigger, though, with due thought for not alerting everyone on the boat, and those ashore, whooping it up at War-Path Landing. Instead, with a twist of the other wrist which brought the .44's butt-plate up and forward, he struck. His target was just behind the fellow's ear, with the blow drawn a trifle; to crush the mastoid bone there usually meant a funeral, and while Lassiter did not give much of a damn for any man who would strip and maul a woman, he preferred to know a bit more about the why and wherefore of the assault before committing himself to a killing.

He was right on target. The man's eyes had started to go wide at the grip of that fist, at sight of Lassiter's hard-planed face — contrasted with his own black beard — and the lift of the .44, but he was granted no time to react or to cry out. The gun's butt crunched against his skull, those eyes rolled up and he fell toward Lassiter, who stepped aside and let him smash deck planking with his face.

3

A moment of some quiet ensued, though the noise ashore seemed to grow louder. Mountain distilled red-eye was being peddled at a buck for a glassful there, as fast as it could be ladled out, and men were standing in line for the somewhat grimy favors of several tarts who were earning their way up-river to the boomtowns of the diggings, Gold Key, Bullhide and Plumas.

Lassiter glanced at the woman. She stood rigidly, hands at her sides, making no attempt to cover herself, either in a state of shock at her mauling or else not caring about her near nakedness.

Shapely feet and legs, he noticed, but why in the devil had she come out of her stateroom wearing only the nightgown? Likely, the man had dragged her out, for his harshly profane charges, with full intent to hurl her over the rail to her death in the swift, merciless current of the Kiskadee. One might possibly fight that torrent of water and swim, stay afloat, but precipitous canyon walls, extending for miles downriver, made escaping alive seem impossible.

About four hours ago, the woman had come aboard, carrying a single bag, with the master of this rickety stern-wheeler sweeping off his cap and bowing low, a pot-bellied clownish man of bristling ginger whiskers and flaming-red nose. "Mrs. Follard, ma'am! Welcome aboard! I'm Cap'n Isaac Strunk, as you might recall from your previous trip up-river with me; that would be two years back, the Colonel was with you then, and let me say at once how sad the loss of him was!"

"Thank you," she had said, eyes lowered, but not before Lassiter, looking on, had noticed they were a smoky shade of gray. "If you will show me to my stateroom, please — ?"

Follard. Lassiter had heard more about her from Anson Brett in Denver. She was a widow for about a year, showing no trace of mourning in a light gray traveling suit as she followed Cap'n Strunk forward.

Even in that suit, the thrust of her

5

limbs had indicated the full thighs and tapering legs now fully on view by starlight and faint moonlight on the deck at a time that was close to midnight.

Lassiter had thought, at that first glimpse of her, that a woman who had lost her husband a year ago should, in the event she had mourned him to any extent at all, be ripe, maybe overly so, for a man to end her period of abstinence. If so, he had meant to find out soon, probably this night, and most likely by overt invasion of her stateroom.

So his thinking had gone, but of course it had not included anything like the murderous assault on her, an occurrence to be capitalized on, at once.

However, he hesitated for a moment, thinking of the bearded man's harsh charges against her — but shrugged and shook off such reminders, and he moved to put his hands on her, on trembling arms and then on the warmth and throbbing of uncovered body flesh.

"Come along," Lassiter said. "I'll take you inside."

She give him a look that seemed dazed and uncomprehending. "Who — are you?" she breathed. But, before he could reply, her glance shifted to the inert figure of the man at their feet; she shuddered and said, "Is he — dead — ?"

"No," Lassiter replied.

"Then kill him!" she whispered. "Now — fast!"

The venom in her voice, the strained, distorted lines of her features, were startling. She thrust herself at Lassiter, close against him. She clawed his arm. "I'll go anywhere with you, do anything, but kill him, a bullet in his head, and then throw him in the river!"

She used lilac perfume. The appeal of all that she was, so overtly offered, so overtly displayed, had a very strong pull. But Lassiter stepped back, breaking the contact between them. "Why?" he demanded. "What's your reason for wanting him dead?"

She did not reply. Staring down at the

7

fellow sprawled on the deck, she lifted a fist to her teeth, gnawed at her knuckles. After a moment she whispered, "Do it! He tried to kill me — I don't owe him anything — !"

Lassiter sent a look both ways along the deck, saw no one. His glance touched the rear corner of the cabin structure on this upper deck, a dozen feet away, then shifted back. "No dice, lady — unless you're ready to give me his name and also a real good reason why he ought to go into the river — "

In this instant, still speaking, someone came around that cabin corner, crouched low, running straight at him, hitting with a driving shoulder which took him just at the knees.

Granted no whisper of warning, bare feet silent against the deck, it was a moment that could have been the last of Lassiter's life, for he was lifted by that shoulder and for a perilous instant he almost went over the rail.

Almost, but not quite, which was all that counted. Perhaps a habit, so long practiced it was instinctive, of always standing well balanced, saved him. Also, slammed against the rail, he managed to wedge himself there, to set himself for handling this attacker.

Which, it was instantly evident, might be quite a job of work. There was a feel of someone young, hickory-tough, whippy-quick in his movements, squirming and twisting, trying to set himself for another driving thrust that would jolt Lassiter off the boat into the icy current.

Face close against Lassiter's, he jeered, "Pray, you buttinsky bastard! You've got just a couple of quick minutes before Satan is squeezing your soul at hell's front door — !"

He was all bony elbows, shoulders, knees, inflicting punishment like a buzzsaw gone berserk. Cramped, his .44 momentarily neutralized, Lassiter reflected acidly that he had been in better situations. And then it got even worse, for the fellow he had laid out with that crunching blow to the mastoid bone, suddenly scrambled about, surged to his feet, breathed gustily and came to lend a hand. He slammed the woman aside, and said, "Let me at him, Suggs; I'm going to stomp his face to jelly!"

His hard, blunt fingers reached to stab at the eyes of Lassiter, who swore in exasperation, his anger flaring, just managing not to lose his head. He lashed out at them, attempting to get his gun free, no matter how, and to gun down both men.

Such precipitate action was a good way for a man to get himself killed. This was a time to exercise the utmost control, to keep icily calm — and to pick without fail exactly the right way to deal out this pair in a hurry, before that bearded one with the hard head began to make good on his threat to stomp a face to jelly.

First step, Lassiter thought, was to cut the odds, somehow, so he would have to deal with only one at a time.

He got a grip on the one called Suggs, rammed the fellow between himself and that other man, so that for a second, a run of precious seconds, they were tangled together, both unable to get in a blow at Lassiter.

Second step, get rid of one of them, and, since Suggs was the closest, pick him.

Suggs was also jammed against Lassiter, who was in turn pinned against the rail; but Suggs twisted violently, an effort to face about, slam into him again. Lassiter had a fleeting impression of a long jaw, jutting brows, cheekbones skinned by recent fights and scarred by old ones. No hat and he had rather long, lank strands of hair.

He also had an impression of the woman, down on one knee, back of hand to mouth, doing nothing to help. In his experience, to count on any woman to act, to do anything at such a time, was the height of wishful folly.

The other man lunged, trying to get around Suggs and to strike again at Lassiter. "Let me at him!" the man gasped.

"No, I've got the son of a bitch set up, sir; you can start stomping him in just a second," Suggs said with his last breath. An instant later he was dead.

It had happened as a result of one of three moves Lassiter had considered; and was set up by a shift in Suggs' stance. For a clock's tick, perhaps, he was vulnerable. It was more than enough for Lasssiter. He dropped his .44 to clear both hands; he seized Suggs, a palm under his chin, fingers twining in his hair. Then he twisted the young hellion's head with a sharp, twisting jerk.

There was a snapping sound like a tree branch breaking. Suggs uttered a shuddering moan as, neck broken, life began to rush out of him. Lassiter put all of his strength into a lift and thrust. Suggs flew over the rail, fell perhaps twenty feet, hit the river with no perceptible splash, seeming to slide gently under the dark, rushing current.

Lassiter turned on the other one with a pivoting move and the swing of a forearm which took him hard under the chin. It staggered the man and drove him back a step. Lassiter, bending, scooped up his own .44 again, then went at the fellow to pistol-whip from him an explanation of the whole incident.

It was a mistake; he should have pulled the trigger and laid him flat on the deck, then conducted the questioning, even if others on the boat tried to horn in. He realized this as the woman suddenly lifted herself and ran at Lassiter, crowding close, pinning his arms.

She was at him for a second only, with some sort of breathless cry, but it was enough, since the other man put a hand to the rail and went over it also.

There was muskiness in Lassiter's nostrils, plus the lilac scent, and feverish body heat under his hands. He threw her aside, lunged at the rail. He saw nothing, nobody. The lower deck jutted out below this one. It was conceivable the man had dropped to it, scuttling aside under cover. Or — he had gone into the river.

From forward in the boat there was a call, "Hey! What's going on back there?"

Footsteps were heading this way.

Lassiter wheeled away from the rail. The woman was starting to move, stumbling uncertainly forward. Lassiter reached to grab her. She fought against him but weakly. He hauled her aside with him, a step and another step, to his own stateroom door; he jerked that open, shoved her inside, followed, closed the door, stood beside it, .44 in fist.

He had left a bracket lamp burning, turned low. She shrank back from him, huddling on a narrow lower bunk, knees drawn up, trying to gather the ragged bits of her nightgown. Lassiter touched the muzzle of his gun to his lips, warning, "Keep quiet. Don't make a sound!"

Footsteps approached, stopped. Somebody said, "Sure thought I heard a couple of jokers scuffling."

More footsteps sounded above, on the texas or wheel-house deck. Cap'n Isaac Strunk said, "You sure it wasn't somebody trying to bother Mrs. Follard?"

"She ain't making no complaint, if so," the other man, now outside of Lassiter's door, replied. "You want I should knock at her stateroom and ask?"

"No," Strunk decided. "She might be having herself a beauty sleep, even if she don't need it much. You just go get ready to handle those drunks when they come yowling aboard."

Both sets of footsteps went away.

Lassiter put the .44 back under his belt. He unbuttoned his shirt and peeled it off. He moved to a small cracked mirror over a wash bowl and pitcher for a look at himself. He saw a faint bruise on one cheek, a purplish blotch over his ribs on the left side, a ragged contusion on his chest.

Then he turned. The woman was starting to slide off the lower bunk as though hoping to make it to and through the door. She paused, for a hurried moistening of lips. "I demand that you let me go! If you don't — I'll scream!"

Discounting this threat, he studied her with pleasure at sight of such opulent feminine contours, so beguilingly revealed.

Her given name, he knew from Anson

Brett, was Amy. She was the widow of a Colonel Jason Follard, Class of '70 at West Point, a man who, a bit more than a year ago, had apparently managed to lose both his own life and approximately two hundred thousand dollars belonging to the U.S. Army — or the money had been stolen, though if so there was no evidence as to who had profited.

Leaning down to her, the lilac scent strong again, Lassiter said, "Who was the fellow that wanted you in the river? Why did you want me to kill him?"

Lips tightening, she did not reply.

"And the other one, called Suggs . . . who was he, why was he involved — ?"

She still made no sound. Reaching out, gripping a bare shoulder, Lassiter said, "I'm going to have answers from you. They can come before what I have in mind, or afterwards, but either way you're going to talk."

Perhaps a shiver ran through her, but Amy Follard still refused to speak.

Lassiter settled beside her, then, with a quick, ruthless play of his hands which

16

made his intentions quite clear. She seemed to moan, now, to lean against him, instead of attempting to escape. He captured her lips with his, while beginning to peel away the tatters of her nightgown.

The woman whimpered. The boat shook constantly and erratic shadows were flickering from the lamp. It was shaping up to quite a night, Lassiter decided — and, after enjoying her to the hilt, he meant to have those answers.

2

IN Lassiter's opinion, any time, any place was agreeable for the enjoyment of a desirable woman.

However, he did have a liking for unusual locales and circumstances, since they seemed to linger longer and more pleasurably in memory. This night's romp with the statuesque beauty, Amy Follard, fell decidedly into the category of the unusual.

The boat shivered constantly, the lamp guttered, flickering low, and the woman cried out, wailed, thrashed, chewing at her under-lip, as he assaulted her in the stateroom bunk, which seemed to have been made with rather small people in mind.

Amy was a glitter of snowy flesh and a tangle of brown hair. A harder glitter came from her eyes, though whether in hate or gratification it was hard to say. Not that Lassiter cared greatly. Gun in fist, the iron indenting the plush hip of the woman — for him, a precautionary practice which seldom varied — he took her as much to establish forceful dominance, on this occasion, than for any other reason.

He assaulted her with his usual hard fury, in his conviction that women in their secret thoughts desired to be roughly used.

In the case of Amy Follard, with her stifled wailing in his ear as the bunk creaked and as cornhusks in the mattress rustled loudly, he formed several quick conclusions.

As he had figured might happen, there was a swift response to him. She was a woman of slumbering passion which came alive — of not much expertise, which suggested not much love by her dead husband. And Lassiter also thought her perhaps a weak, soft sort of woman, but then he began to wonder, with a growing hunch there might be someone else; hard, hidden, watchful, playing an adroit game all her own behind the pretty, sensually alluring facade.

He put this aside for consideration later and finished it. Then, both of them rather moist from their exertions, a fine tremor in the woman still, her eyes squeezed shut just before the lamp flickered out, he put his hands on her, clamped hard, and began his questions again concerning the pair who had tried for his life and hers as well.

This time, answers came readily, as though she had turned the matter over in her mind, deciding to talk — or she had utilized the time fabricating lies to tell him. "Suggs was a private at Fort Furlong in Montana when my husband commanded there. He was assigned for a short time as his batman, to look after his uniform, shine his boots, do various chores about our quarters. I hadn't seen him in more than a year, but — recognized him."

"So. And the other one — ?"

"That was Clyde Mungo. He was at Furlong also. He was an Indian trader."

Lassiter remembered Anson Brett, in Denver, saying that money from several trading posts might have been lost along with the government cash being convoyed by Follard.

He said, "So why does Mungo go for you? Why Suggs?"

She countered with a question of her own, "Have you h-heard of what happened at the Horsehead Crossing of Brule River a year ago last May?"

"Seems I have, somewhere, but tell me anyway."

"My husband went into the river, trying to save the rig that was lost, the one with the — the money. He was drowned. His body was never recovered. But Mungo doesn't believe it happened that way. He thinks I have the money — or that I know where it is. And he wants it, will kill anybody to get it. As for Suggs, I suppose he has thrown in with Mungo."

Somehow, it didn't quite seem to fit, though for a reason that had nothing to do with her words. Lassiter groped for

21

that reason, but could not pin it down.

He stood up, went to open the stateroom door and let some air in. Brilliant stars speckled a segment of black sky above the canyon. Various noises came from the other side of the boat, where those passengers who had sampled the dreary delights ashore were stumbling back aboard. Some probably wouldn't make it, would be left behind when the *Aurora* headed on up-river tomorrow.

Amy Follard spoke again. "I went home to my people in Maryland. But after 5 years of Army posts, this is my country now; I intend to live in it, which is why I am coming back. But Mungo was suddenly here tonight, saying I returned to pick up the money . . ."

Her voice trailed off. It still didn't fit. Mungo must not know where the money was, or he would have it — and it seemed highly unlikely he would have risked killing the woman, if he suspected she knew its whereabouts, before moving to squeeze that information from her.

Lassiter went to the stand under the

mirror, poured water into the bowl and began to wash up. Over his shoulder, he said, "Well, I can understand now why you wanted me to stick a bullet in his head — a reasonable enough reaction after what he tried to do to you — "

In truth, he wasn't buying much of anything she had said. Still to be told was her account of how she had happened to be on deck in only her nightgown, waiting to be mauled by Mungo. Lassiter rather anticipated hearing the story she would offer to explain that.

But the question which would prod her to explain was not asked, for Amy Follard was suddenly gone, darting out of Lassiter's stateroom, then the door of her own stateroom opening and closing. What was left of her nightgown had gone with her.

Lassiter smiled thinly. He had offered her the opportunity to run, wondering if she would seize it and she had. It was another odd piece to fit into the jigsaw puzzle he was assembling.

Pulling on his gear, he left the

stateroom also, moved back along the deck to a dark shadow cast by the boat's paddles. There he settled himself and waited. If Clyde Mungo had survived that leap over the rail, if he came again to this deck tonight, Lassiter meant to serve as a welcoming committee of one.

Waiting, he reviewed in detail what had happened in Denver four days ago.

Not in very great detail, though, where his encounter with Stag Durkee was concerned, for that seemed wholly accidental — a boisterous hello from Stag, who worked business deals similar to those Lassiter liked to tackle, and then a visit to his room at the Brown Palace Hotel. Stag was a big, burly man with a shock of iron-gray hair, seamed features, and always perched on his knee, one of the decorative young females he accumulated.

That female was what Lassiter remembered best about the visit paid Stag in his room. She had flaming red hair, softly formed lips, very pale skin that looked as supple as velvet, and greenish cat eyes. An expensive young woman, Lassiter had decided. He would have liked to take her off Stag's hands. "Hey, you got anything laid on, boy? Then how about tackling a job for me, down near Cananea?" Stag had asked.

Amused at being called boy, though Stag did have a good dozen years on him, Lassiter had said, "No, thanks. I'm thinking of taking a pasear up to the Kiskadee country."

This was after his talk with Anson Brett, and he had already decided to go and look for the big bundle of cash Colonel Jason Follard supposedly had lost.

Squinting at him, Stag had said, "Whyever in the hell for? That squib of a boom up there? I had a report on it — due to fizzle out almost any minute. Down at Cananea, now, I'm holding an option to buy a mountain that's mostly pure silver, with all kinds of pesty thieves trying to steal it. Go and sit on that for me, keep the lid down, until I can dicker a sale of the whole shebang. A fourth of the gross take to you, boy; it'll keep you in fillies and brandy for years!"

Lassiter had said no. He had already reached his agreement with Anson Brett, and anyway he had had enough of Mexico for a while, really wanted to see a different kind of country. Besides which . . . well, he would want no better man siding him in a fight with all the chips down than Stag Durkee, but he did not wholly trust him otherwise.

Fondling a glossy thigh under a very short skirt as the red-haired girl on his knee watched Lassiter with what seemed to be bored indifference, Stag had grumbled at his decision. "Damn it, I'll have to go handle the Cananea deal myself — or let it slide." Then, squinting again at him, "Listen, I never knew you to be one for just taking sightseeing trips. You got something good going for you, up the Kiskadee? Because, whatever it is, I'll buy in, and you name the price!"

But Lassiter had fobbed him off. He had promised Anson Brett to keep all they had talked about completely private. Regretting he had not made a try to take the red-head off Stag's hands, Lassiter thought again of his talk with that other man in Denver.

A quiet, trap-mouthed sort, Anson Brett, who held a position high up the ladder in Washington. The reason Lassiter was in Denver was that Brett had sent twenty telegrams to as many places where he might be, asking for a meeting. One had reached him in St. Louis, where he was en route west anyway, from New Orleans and Natchez — rather slowly, playing poker here and there, doing quite well.

His bankroll was fat; he doubted that he would be interested in whatever Brett wanted him to do. But the story that Brett told was so bizarre that his interest was seized and held immediately.

The government had decided to close a string of forts in the northwest. Built originally for cavalry action against the Sioux and the Blackfeet, they were no longer needed, as those fighting tribes had been subdued for some time now.

An Army ambulance with a guard of twelve troopers, commanded by Colonel Follard, had headed eastward from Fort Trimble in northern Idaho. Its cargo was government money, more than two hundred thousand dollars, to handle closing-out payrolls and other expenses, at each fort as it was reached.

On the way, the ambulance was to pick up additional cash at Indian trading posts which were being closed also. By the time disaster struck, Brett had said, they might have garnered as much as fifty thousand.

Disaster had occurred at the Horsehead Crossing of Brule River, a turbulent mountain stream just north of where it flowed into the Kiskadee. The ambulance had slid off a road into the river. Colonel Follard had somehow been swept to his death with the rig. Or — had it happened that way at all?

"Mrs. Follard was along in another rig. It was sort of a second honeymoon for those two," Brett had said. "But she was some distance away at the time. So were all but two of the troopers. One of those, the ambulance driver, turned up missing, no doubt drowned also. The other disappeared, later, after telling several different stories of what occurred."

Suggs, perhaps — ? Lassiter wondered. And where had Mungo been at the time?

Brett, continuing, had said, "The Brule runs deep near that crossing. No trace of the wagon was found, nor Follard's body, though a search began at once and continued for several days. Mrs. Follard was grief-stricken. She apparently left almost at once to go back to her people in the east. The matter seemed to be at an end, a complete loss. Another shipment of cash would have to be sent for closing those forts. But — "

He paused. And Lassiter said, "Yes. Some of the money supposedly lost in Brule River began to show up."

Brett started. "My God, how did you know?"

29

"I didn't." Lassiter stood, began to pace Brett's hotel room. "I'm guessing. However, you sent those telegrams, you want me to go up the Kiskadee and look around — and that must be the reason."

Brett nodded. "The numbers of all bills, twenty dollars and above, were recorded, and banks everywhere were notified to be on the lookout for them, just in case. And, as you remarked, a few of them have turned up. Scattered from hell to breakfast — or more literally, from Chicago to Seattle, and I had a wire yesterday that a couple of them also appeared at a bank in El Paso."

"Money travels," Lassiter commented. "A man receives some bills in change, rides a train for five hundred miles, spends them when he gets off. You think, though, that the bulk of that lost cash is still up there, somewhere close, in all likelihood, to where it was supposedly lost?"

"Er — yes," Brett replied.

"So do I. If it had been split up, all

those involved handed a share, the bills that were recovered would be showing up in quantity, since spending them would begin quick. Some of it is being spread now — only some — indicating somebody needs to dip into that cash every now and then."

"So hopefully most of it is still intact somewhere," Brett said, "and can be recovered."

"Which brings us to the meat of the matter," Lassiter said. "How much to me for getting it back?"

Eyes abruptly hooded, Brett said, "Ten percent."

Lassiter snorted. "Try again! Twenty-five!"

"My God, I can't sell that figure in Washington!"

"Nobody in Washington is risking his hide in such a hunt, neither are you. I am, and I mean to be paid well for taking such a risk," Lassiter said.

"I might be able to get you twelve and a half."

"Twenty. No less than that, and your

firm word the pay-off will be at that figure — or else hand me right now what I laid out in travel and expenses, St. Louis to Denver, answering the wires you sent, and call it quits."

Brett protested. He fumed and pleaded, mopping his brow. But he capitulated, promising a twenty percent pay-off.

He was a man riding a razor, Lassiter thought, strong pressure on him to do something about that missing money, and in a quandary as to what should be done, trying to find it in wild country, hundreds of miles of that raw wilderness still. An Army might find it — or one man might.

Brett had chosen the latter course, hiring Lassiter to try. He must now wait and do some anxious sweating, likely with the thought that the odds were against Lassiter succeeding, a wild goose chase, a high gamble probably against even him coming back alive.

And maybe all that was true, Lassiter thought, standing watch by night on the cabin deck of the river-boat *Aurora*, with the growl of the untamed Kiskadee loud in the darkness. But he liked high bets, and the thought of collecting thirty thousand dollars or so was a potent lure, indeed.

Also, it might run to more than that. He had not mentioned collecting on the money from the Indian trading posts, if there was any. Neither had Brett. There could be an even higher pay-off, if he got his hands on that cash.

If it did turn into a wild goose chase, there was some recompense already in his meeting of Amy Follard.

Lassiter thought of her during the cold black dawn hours at the bottom of the deep high country canyon with the river singing its savage song. She was the kind of woman he liked — shapely, intriguing, with questions about her. Who knew what game she might be playing? He liked above all that she was no prim, proper lady when brought to bed.

He discounted that her husband might still be alive, which was a possibility, though a very faint one; he could not picture a man with such a woman letting her run loose, to be taken by such as Lassiter.

Then he stiffened alertly. Somebody had come onto the deck and was moving this way, almost as quietly as a drifting shadow.

Since there were only four staterooms, two on either side of the boat, the prowler's objective had to be Lassiter's room — or that of Amy Follard.

Lassiter started toward him with silent sliding steps. The prowler stopped, hissed faintly and pulled trigger at him — there was the snap of a hand-gun, red gust of powderflame, and a quick shift of his position while firing.

With a parallel movement, Lassiter squeezed trigger in response. There was a savage bark of the .44. He moved right, hugging the cabin structure corner. The other's bullet had been a narrow miss — cat-eyes in him, Lassiter surmised, but he had sharp night vision himself, and when the fellow pulled the trigger at him again, a baleful flare of gunfire showed the dark bulk of his body, and with another bullet Lassiter hit him.

It was a low hit, maybe only a leg-rip, raising a snarl and a sideward stumble which rammed him against the rail. Lassiter ran at him, free hand reaching, gripping a muscle-corded shoulder, his gun swinging to lay him out. He wanted some answers, either to clarify or disprove what Amy Follard had said, and this seemed a good place to begin.

But the man squirmed in his grip, as quick and wriggly as an eel, and the smell of him, strong and rank in the night, told eloquently what he was.

It was a smell compounded of wood smoke, animal blood and guts, and grease, all impregnating a body that might well never have been washed by soap and hot water. It was the sort of smell to be encountered in some Indian villages.

Lassiter, who had known many such

35

Indians, realized he had caught a buck, but probably not of the Blackfoot, Nez Perce, or any of the Sioux tribes, since those proud warrior people did not let themselves smell so rank. More likely, this was one from the brutalized, degraded river tribes along the Kiskadee, Salmon, and Snake Rivers. Even having caught him, he was in danger of losing his catch. But the swing of his gun also scored a hit, and with a cat-like snarl the buck fell back against the rail once more.

He hung there a second as Lassiter shifted his feet and moved quickly for another strike, but before he could act, the Indian went over the rail in a fluid, lizard-like squirm, dropping as Clyde Mungo had, but with a sudden frantic howl which indicated he had missed the lower deck and had gone into the river.

Then there was quiet, except for several drowsy, profane yells in protest against the racket.

Lassiter shook his head, displeased but

accepting. The toll in blood demanded by that missing money was mounting up. Now it behooved him to move with exceptional care lest his own blood be spilled also.

3

IN bright morning sunlight the *Aurora* beat its way slowly up-river, shaken in every joint by the pounding current, its paddles beating the water to snowy froth. Cap'n Isaac Strunk manned the wheel, sweating anxiously as he scanned riffles ahead that warned of hidden rocks. There were numerous twists and turns in the deep-walled river canyon, usually with stretches of rapids, and the boat had to claw its way through those, with the half-naked black crew-man at the bow constantly casting the lead and calling depths.

Lassiter had dozed off towards five and slept fairly late. When he rose he shaved quickly and deftly then he folded the razor and tucked it in the top of his right boot. In the dining salon of cracker-box dimensions, he breakfasted on ham, hominy grits with red-eyed gravy, soda biscuits and coffee whose bitterness was slightly relieved by blackstrap molasses.

After breakfast he moved down a stairway to the lower deck and began a head by head check of every soul on board. If an Indian with last night's smell, limping on a leg with a bullet in it might possibly be a fellow passenger, he meant to know this — and he was also looking for anyone with a black beard.

His search turned up neither of them.

A strange miscellany of passengers rode the *Aurora* — greenhorns who sat as sullenly fearful guards over the astonishing piles of junk they were taking to the diggings and seedy tinhorns, ragged of gear, who were trying to stir up business by dealing greasy cards on dirty blankets.

The tarts who had dispensed their favors ashore during last night's lay-over sat together, listlessly studying mirrors, poking at dull faces and frowsy hair. They were a dreary looking lot after the night's debauchery. They perked up at the sight of Lassiter, rightly gauging with the sharpness of their ilk that his gear indicated a sizable roll. With simpers and beguiling glances they vainly attempted to stir his interest.

Lassiter thought of Amy Follard. He had not seen her again and presumed she was still in her state-room. Continuing to think of her, he paused at the bow, studying the curling feathers of white ahead which warned of granite fangs that might rip the belly out of this frail craft, though apparently Cap'n Strunk knew his business — indeed, for several years had made the trip from the town of LeGrande up the river and back.

Lassiter had decided to begin his search at LeGrande. There were several other ways to reach the diggings — trails through the mountains on both sides of the Kiskadee — but they were slow and tiring. The quickest way was by this boat.

He had told Anson Brett, "I'll likely know within days whether the money can be recovered. If you want a personal report from me — maybe delivery of the cash — follow along to that town of LeGrande and wait there."

Starting back along the deck, Lassiter thought of Amy Follard's coming aboard yesterday at that huddle of shacks called War Path Landing. A stage ran to it every now and then from some branch line rail town in Montana, he had heard, and also the *Aurora* always stopped at War Path Landing to pass the night and to load up on the chunks of pine which its engines burned.

Was there a reason why the woman had chosen to board the boat there, rather than at LeGrande? Lassiter considered it, with a mental note to squeeze her for an answer when they met again.

His attention was on the canyon walls. The east wall was shallowing down, off to northward, and a stretch of fairly flat country was beginning to appear, when someone spoke to him with acid sharpness. "Look out where you're putting your big clodhoppers, you whopper-jawed stupid jackass!"

It jerked him abruptly back to the

present, and to a person sitting on a spread-out blanket, swinging the muzzle of an old Henry rifle. The voice apparently belonged to a female, a young one trying to talk big and succeeding fairly well, and a study of her gear seemed to confirm the impression. At least, she wore a skirt but her grimy bare legs and feet, a man's hat crammed down on a shock of black hair, cut raggedly short, and an elkhide vest, all made her gender look dubious.

But then she spoke again. Her voice was an angry twang but it was undoubtedly feminine. "And stop staring at me! Haul out! Make tracks or I'll notch an ear for you!"

Lassiter frowned. He lifted a boot, used it to shove the rifle barrel aside. "Point your blunderbuss somewhere else, sis," he said, "or it's liable to wind up at the bottom of the river."

"I'm not your sis!" she snapped. "Not anybody's — and you try taking my long gun, it's the last thing you'll ever be trying!"

An old man's cackle sounded nearby.

"Heh-heh! You think she's only hoorawing you? Listen, Mister, you better back off like she says, or you'll have a bloody stump where you're now wearing an ear — either ear, though she's kind of partial to the right side one!"

Lassiter saw a skinny oldster, standing incongruously buttoned up on this hot morning in an Army greatcoat, once black, now shiny green with age. His head, like a turtle's, stuck out at the top, and not only his head but his bony face was totally devoid of any follicle of hair.

Sucking at his toothless gums, and with a beak of a nose and a lack of chin contributing to his turtle-like appearance, he continued, "I'm Lonzo Moots, so by God old I traipsed these hills once with the likes of Jim Bridger and Kit Carson — and her, she's my great-granddaughter, Effie."

Lassiter frowned and wrinkled his nostrils, but the odor in the air was decidedly different from the one last night. Still, it was of a kind he did not like, that of unbathed female. "A word of advice to you, old man . . . wash her! Use lye soap and a stiff bristled brush, if one is handy — scrub hard, even if an outer layer of hide peels off — "

"Heh-heh!" Lonzo Moots said, but uneasily.

"Why, you goddam cottonmouth crud!" Effie Moots cried in a voice half-strangled by rage. The muzzle of her rifle whipped at him. Her finger was on the trigger.

A gun cracked, and a bullet was a hornet-whine inches from Lassiter's face, but it was not the girl's rifle that had fired. With a corner of his eye, he caught a gush of grayish-black powdersmoke coming from his right, a little back from the Kiskadee north bank where it shallowed down.

The distance was less than a hundred yards, not much of a marksmanship test for a skilled man with a good rifle. Lassiter was a good target, standing on this lower deck, forward, the sunshine bright on him — and likely only an abrupt dip of the boat had saved him.

44

The man who had squeezed trigger was also in plain view. It was the black-bearded fellow of last night, Clyde Mungo. Instead of lining another sight fast, though, and firing another bullet with the slight correction that might insure a hit, he was turning away, running heavily to a horse waiting nearby, hauling himself into the saddle.

A second man was visible, coming at a trot, then wheeling his mount, and the two came together. The second man handed over another rifle and the bearded fellow took it. He had probably used a single-shot weapon, Lassiter thought — maybe a Springfield.

All of this happened very fast, and a good part of it was occurring as Lassiter bent down and took the Henry rifle from the girl's hands. This was not done easily; she was hissing and spitting at him, showing, up close, a round face, a faintly snub nose, and large blue eyes, features that could be pretty when not distorted by rage. Lassiter tore the rifle from her grasp as she tried earnestly to rake open his face with her nails.

He whipped away from her, a step, another step. He lifted the rifle, finding it — and what else to expect, a gun hauled around by a woman? — with a loose, rather rickety feel, but nevertheless he lined a sight of his own, while swiftly estimating wind and range. Then he had to wait out the almost rhythmic up-and-down motion of the *Aurora* for the boat to reach a crest and hold there for several seconds before he squeezed trigger.

Meanwhile, the bearded man was settling to his own aim for a second shot. He would likely, Lassiter thought, be the first to fire. In actuality the two rifles cracked almost simultaneously, with the Henry perhaps a fractional instant ahead of the one ashore.

Lassiter did not even hear the second bullet that came at him. It was an even wider miss. His own slug, the heavy chunk of lead fired from the Henry's .50 calibre cartridge, spent itself in a wholly unexpected manner. The second fellow ashore, beyond and to the right of the bearded man, folded, then pitched from his saddle to sprawl inertly on the ground.

The Henry was the carbine model, which carried eight cartridges in the magazine, but when Lassiter hurriedly flipped its lever and aimed again, picking up the bearded man, now bent low on his horse and spurring it hard, when he swiftly adjusted, compensating for that throw to the right, only a dry click sounded. Only one cartridge had been in the gun.

He had concentrated wholly on this murderous business, and it had run its course in a minute or less — but time enough, he saw, glancing about, to attract considerable attention. There was already a crowd of people staring at him gape-mouthed.

Lassiter gave them a look which made the whole crowd fall back. He handed the Henry to Effie Moots, now on her feet, hands out to snatch the rifle back. "It throws to the right, maybe as much as a foot for every hundred feet of range," Lassiter told her.

She brandished the rifle in one hand as though to swing its barrel at his head. Then she used language on Lassiter that he had seldom before heard from feminine lips, and certainly not from any female who, in all likelihood, was not yet as much as fifteen. The very air seemed to crackle and turn purple. She expressed the opinion that his mother had been a mangy bitch and his father a scrofulous hound, she invited him with passion to commit an unspeakable and impossible act upon himself, and she tried again to claw his face.

Gripping a handful of the elkhide vest to hold her off, Lassiter glanced to Lonzo Moots, who was heh-hehing again. Perhaps he was so addled he cackled at everything. "Sounds like she was raised in a filthy pig lot behind a pretty foul sporting house," Lassiter commented. "When you give her that bath, wash out her mouth, too — and use the same lye soap for it."

When Lassiter let go of her, the girl went sprawling against Lonzo Moots. He fell with her on top of him. This, especially the furious scissoring of her legs, brought attention again from the onlookers, even though she wore linen drawers, with — an unexpected touch — lace and ribbons at her knees. Lassiter wheeled away, heading aft. The boat was already past the spot where the man ashore had fallen. The one with the beard had disappeared, and it seemed obvious he was not going to turn back to his companion who had stopped Lassiter's bullet.

This suspicion was confirmed by his sudden reappearance on a ridge yonder. He had picked up still another rider and the two of them were visible for a moment before turning away, going over the ridge crest and out of sight, though Lassiter paused and watched for several minutes.

There had been something of an inward ripple of recognition; a woman sat saddle with a certain subtle difference, and for a bet that second rider had been female.

Lassiter climbed the stairway to the cabin deck. He was hailed by Cap'n Strunk, looking down at him from the texas. "What was that shooting all about?" the master of the *Aurora* demanded.

"Maybe you can tell me," Lassiter responded.

"How in the hell should I know? Damned few trips, either way, I deliver all the passengers that come aboard, usually because of bullets flying somewhere, along the way. I heard some last night, back aft, the side of the boat for the state-room you paid for, and was kind of surprised to see you up and around this morning. Kept my nose out, though; I learned years ago to do that, leaving other folks business alone, especially the kind that might mean promiscuous lead-throwing — "

For emphasis, he tapped a finger against his nose, the magnificent crimson proboscis that could have been acquired only by drinking thousands of gallons of whiskey — and probably impressive quantities of brandy, gin and anything else potable, as well.

"Tell you one thing, though, for what it might be worth, I got a pretty good look at the jasper trying to throw down on you, and think maybe I know him. Somebody mean as a rattler at skin-shedding time and I've got a reason to hate his guts, since he took a woman from me once . . . fellow who used to be in the Indian trading business, on north, name of Clyde Mungo . . ."

Cap'n Strunk's final words seemed to echo slightly, "You meet up with him again, I hope you plug that slimy son plumb center, in the gut — for a long painful dying — !"

Lassiter raised his fist to knock at Amy Follard's door. He hesitated; he pushed gently, and it swung open.

The state-room was empty, save for the tatters of her nightgown, on the floor. Looked as if she had left and likely not in a leap over the rail, since the bag which had come aboard with her was gone also. She must have left at dawn when Lassiter was dozing.

He paid tribute to her ability to depart unobserved. Then he contemplated what seemed a plain fact — she was now riding with the man who had tried to kill her last night and whom she had begged Lassiter to kill. Damn it! What was going on?

No answer of any kind to the question came to Lassiter as the day wore along. But it seemed mandatory that learning the answer must be high on his list of things to be done at journey's end.

The high-booming river town of Plumas was raucously noisy at twilight as the *Aurora*, after some miles of relatively smooth going, moved alongside a wharf to tie up. Just forward of it was what appeared to be a twenty-foot naphtha launch which exuded a smell of half-burned coal oil.

Lassiter, with no luggage to hamper him, was the first one ashore, leaping deftly from deck to wharf.

Striding along a dirt street that was slick with mud from an afternoon shower, he thought momentarily of Lonzo Moots and his contrary great-granddaughter, wrestling odd-shaped bundles across the deck for disembarking. Somebody had remarked that they followed the peddling trade, visiting isolated ranches and small hamlets in a rickety wagon.

Plumas was a town of many guns, Lassiter noticed, of heavy wagons hauled by straining horses, of much excited talk concerning the latest news from Bullhide and Gold Key, the settlements closest to the new strikes, off to westward. Lassiter, who had known other boomtowns, was not stirred by such talk. Perhaps one man in a thousand ever struck it rich, and he regarded such odds as far too high to buck.

Checking first for a room he counted off five saloons and three whorehouses before finding the town hotel, the only structure in Plumas of more than one story. When he inquired there he was informed by a supercilious clerk that not only were no rooms available, but there was a waiting list too prohibitively long for him even to bother adding another name to it.

But two twenties, shifted from Lassiter's roll to the clerk's palm, brought a swift change. There might be a room available, he decided — his own, on the ground floor, at the back, but for only one night. Lassiter took its key.

Next, at the general store, he spread more cash, shopping first for a holster for his .44. This had to be chosen with care and a dozen draws to make sure of no leather cramp. He drew at medium speed but still fast enough to make several onlookers blink. There was no shellbelt in stock; he had to settle for cartridges shoved in a jacket pocket.

He also purchased a Winchester .30-.30 and shells for it, gear for himself, several items needed for camping and cooking, grub staples, a couple of blankets.

Going on to a livery stable, he bought a chestnut gelding about sixteen hands high and saddle gear for it, then a broad-beamed bay, warranted to be a good pack animal and pack gear as well — not to carry a load away from Plumas, but for what he hoped to bring back when he returned.

By now it was night. Leaving most of what he had bought at the stable, Lassiter dined at a hole-in-the-wall restaurant with very high prices and indifferent fare. He ate a tough steak and half-raw potatoes, still, he ate heartily — there were possible lean days to come.

He started back toward the hotel, shrugging off several pesty individuals who wanted to detail the incredible delights and ridiculously low prices of the women for whom they were pimping.

Though, he was thinking, the company of a woman tonight would not be at all disagreeable — but one woman in particular — Amy Follard. However, a close check of everybody on the town's streets and a good number of discreet questions had failed to turn up anyone remotely resembling her — or the bearded

Clyde Mungo, either.

It was still early when Lassiter unlocked the rear door of that room at the hotel, stepped inside, and heard an instant rustling sound, accompanied by an agreeable whiff of perfume. He grinned; she had searched for and found him, and he grabbed for her fast, with the heartening sensation of a woman squirming in his arms, gasping something, a plea.

But — a hurried sweep of his hands, here and there, and the sound of her voice . . . informed him that this decidedly was not Amy Follard. Gripping her with one hand, he produced a match, snapped it on a thumb-nail.

What he had caught was the green-eyed red-head he had seen before — perched on Stag Durkee's knee.

"P-please! Let me go!" she gasped.

Lassiter laughed. "Not likely! I've got some plans for you and me, sweetheart — things to do, beginning no more than about a quick minute from now!"

4

WITH the match still burning, Lassiter looked the woman over. She wore a green-and-white checked gingham dress, demure enough but with the contours of her sensuous young body pressing boldly against it — plus a poke bonnet. Her red hair was in pigtails.

Squirming, she said, "You're hurting me! And I'm not going to run away if you let me go — !"

This, of course, was obvious; she had not waited here in the dark for him only to flee now. Nevertheless, Lassiter continued to hold onto her, enjoying her closeness and the enticing scent she used, like some tropical flower. "How in the hell did you get to Plumas so quick?" Then he guessed, "That naptha launch — !"

"Well, yes," she admitted. "Stag bought

it at the town down-river, saying he had to get here first and find out what you were up to; and I thought I would die, the boat bouncing all the time, plus the smell of the coal oil that was brought along to make the engine run. My stomach is still turning over and over."

She shivered. Lassiter blew out the match.

Perhaps it was something he should have anticipated — Stag's move to get here ahead of him. Stag was not one to let the grass grow under his feet when a deal was pending.

"Also," the girl continued, "he was constantly shooting at things, often right past my face, seeing how close he could come without hitting me. He said drinking and shooting were all he could do in front of the man who was steering the boat and making the engine run. Gosh, I was so scared!"

She shivered again.

Lassiter moved sideways to the bed. It creaked loudly as he sat down. He pulled the red-head onto his lap. "So

58

scared you just had to shake loose from Stag and come to me?"

His tone was ironical; he knew that it had not happened that way.

"Oh, no," she replied. "He told me to come here and wait for you — to say he noticed the look in your eyes, at that Denver hotel room, telling how much you would like to get your hands on me — " and this said with a matter of factness acknowledging how much virtually all men would like their hands on her " — so to go ahead, help yourself, and later you and him — would talk — "

Lassiter chuckled. He savored her words and Stag's action. It was typical of the man — a bold, forthright move, perhaps cloaking an attempt to make him bite at some hook with this highly seductive young female as bait.

Finding the snaps and buttons which held her dress closed, he murmured, "What are you called? Red, maybe — ?"

"No, it's Lurie," she replied. "That's short for Allura, which is a name gave me by a Mrs. Fike at a — er — boarding house where I worked for a while, there in Denver. My real name is Prudence Glossop, which Mrs. Fike said was liable to turn men away."

Lassiter, chuckling inwardly and greatly diverted, said, "Well, Lurie, this is a nice dress you're wearing and I'd hate to tear it, so if you'd cooperate just a little — "

Obligingly lifting herself and raising her arms so he could work the dress over her head, Lurie revealed a single sheer garment that was easily removable. "I'm all at once trying to remember the first time this ever happened to me. Years ago when I was about thirteen, I guess."

It didn't seem likely she was more than five or six years older than that now. Her arms coiled gently around his neck, her warm sweet lips offered themselves to him, and her slimness hinted that there was a peak of ripeness yet to come in her.

At the same time, she was an instrument of that bluff, dangerous hellion, Stag Durkee. There was no telling how he meant to use her against Lassiter, and he needed to be on guard against anything and everything.

So, grappling her in his usual driving fashion, Lassiter kept the .44 nearby and maintained a wary watch, all senses alert. The room was fusty and smelled as though its occupant had not bothered to clean it in a month of Sundays. There were clashing odors of hair oil, dirty socks, a sourness of spilled liquor, and the grimy sheets of the abominably squeaking bed.

Lurie sighed, "That's the way Stag does it, too, with a gun in his hand. Well, as long as you don't shoot at anything, right past my face — "

Lassiter half expected that Stag, ever the nonconformist, as addicted to doing the unanticipated, the unforeseen, as was Lassiter himself, might abruptly barge in, to take his jeering pleasure from interrupting the scene here, and, surprising him, then to dicker from behind a gun for what Lassiter knew.

If so, Stag would be the one who

would wind up surprised. Lassiter, with his cat-eyes in the dark, was confident he could beat Stag to the punch, snap a bullet that might not be near Lurie's face but would certainly burn very close to the face of Stag Durkee. He would grant that much leeway to a one-time friend. But the bullet following, if one was necessary, would be aimed at the man's heart.

However, nothing happened, other than an enjoyable thrusting to the ultimate limits of pleasure; there were no signs of danger, only the distant night noises of Plumas and the faint, shaken exclamations of ecstacy from the girl who had been born Prudence Glossop.

Ultimately, both lay still, and there continued to be nothing to indicate any move by Stag Durkee. Maybe it was to be a game of cat and mouse, already begun here, but if Stag thought he, Lassiter, would accept the role of mouse, a disturbing surprise was in store for him.

Quivering from her excesses of passionate

abandon, Lurie sighed, "Golly, I do like to be with a man! Even if it means I'm so wicked I'll go straight to hell — "

Smiling, relishing the fragrance of her as he palmed the satiny texture of her skin, Lassiter said, "Maybe we'll both wind up there. But it might not be so bad, since I have a pretty good idea that that is where most of the interesting people are going to be, too!"

He stood by a window, looking out. It was late, close to midnight, but the street noises persisted. Plumas was a town that went to bed late.

Lassiter was restless. He sensed that he should be out and on the move, not only searching again for Amy Follard and Mungo, but checking on various things that would affect his movements tomorrow.

And, additionally, it was possible he might locate Stag Durkee, discover what he might be doing especially after Stag had heard a report from Lurie. Suddenly there seemed no reason to delay that.

Over his shoulder, he said, "Time to get dressed and be on your way with regret at having to call it quits for now, and also with apologies for not inviting you to spend the night, but I've got things to do."

"Oh, that's all right," Lurie replied. "Stag said you would likely shake me off, saying you had things to do, and that I was to get out of the way."

Lassiter thought, with no attempt by her to find out what he meant to do tomorrow? Then he realized this would be untypical of Stag. He was too clever. And he saw with what he felt was complete clarity just what Stag had actually had in mind in sending the girl here. He had wanted to force an opening move from Lassiter, get him started toward where he was heading, then to follow along.

Watching the girl as she pulled on her undergarment and snugged it down about her hips, he said, "Okay; you tell Stag to buy some good horses and supplies, if he hasn't already, because I'm

64

heading northwest at first light — wild country, rough going, but he comes along or else folds his hand."

Perhaps it was a foolish play, revealing exactly where he meant to go — but it was exactly the type of move Lassiter most enjoyed. The burden was on Stag Durkee now — to figure whether or not he had lied, and, if he had not, the added burden of trying to trail along and keep up. For Lassiter, meant to make it very difficult to stay on his trail.

"All right, I'll tell him," Lurie agreed.

Moving close to him with her charming candor, she offered her lips in a good-bye kiss. "I sure liked it with you," Lurie sighed, "and I'm kind of sorry I can't stay all night. But I'd better get back. Stag has bad headaches, pretty often; he needs me to rub his forehead and make them go away."

She left, then, with a faint sibilant patter of footsteps. A wisp of her perfume lingered in the smelly room.

Lassiter went after her quickly. But, fast as he moved, she had been even faster. Within seconds, he knew Lurie had shaken him off. Perhaps she had done it without meaning to, but on the other hand, he decided, it would be as much of a mistake to down-rate her as to down-rate Stag himself.

So it would have to be only guesswork as to where Stag might be holed up in this town — and, on second thought, maybe it wasn't so important to know. Lassiter felt that by tomorrow he might know too well where the man was . . . on his back trail and perhaps closing fast.

It depended on the moves he made tonight — or on one specific move in particular that had suddenly become mandatory, but that must be delayed for an hour or so while he sought an item of information that he felt he should have, if possible, before leaving the town.

Thinking of this, he started working along the backs of buildings parallel to the long main street of Plumas. His attention was only partially on the street and the buildings he passed, while he considered where he might go, whom he might approach, for the information he wanted.

Ordinarily there would be no problem — approach a bartender, show a bill and pick his brains. Such gentry usually knew all that went on, but Lassiter rather doubted that any Plumas bartender would know what he wanted to know.

After only several moments, he was aware of being followed. There was a tingling at the back of his neck, a tightening of his gut and a coldness along his spine. He sought a shadow, became completely still, and stood waiting. Stag, maybe, or somebody working for Stag — ?

But no one came along, and the sense of being stalked faded. Lassiter shook his head, wondering if it had been a false alarm — bothersome, if true, since he placed considerable dependence and trust in the sixth sense that so often warned him of danger.

He moved on, found himself alongside a pole fence. Beyond it was a fire and someone hunched down, crooning in a cracked, faded voice. A naked pate glittered like a china egg in the nest of a broody hen.

Starting, Lassiter muttered, "I'll be damned!"

His steps might have led him fortuitously onto exactly what he was seeking. Ducking between the poles, he walked across what seemed the rear of a corral. Beyond the fire three or four mules were standing, eyes shining with almost human intelligence. Off to one side there was a sort of lean-to, with a dim glow beyond a canvas wall, likely a candle. At the other side was a wooden watering trough, full and spilling over.

"Evening, Mr. Moots!" Lassiter said.

The head came jerkily about. The old man peered at him. "Heh-heh! Damned few call me Mister, or ever did! Do I know you, maybe?"

"Sure." Lassiter settled on his heels, across the fire, fed a scrap of wood to the flame. "We met on the boat."

He glanced at several packs made up and waiting, stacked nearby on the ground. "Looks like you're ready to pull out."

"Yep. We'll be dangling eastward, come first light — leastways, if I can prod that danged gal out of her blankets. She's as mean as spit early in the morning."

"You won't be heading up toward the Brule?"

"Got no cause to. Pretty empty country up that way. We go where there's folks to trade for the stuff we pack to them."

"But you know the country where the Brule meets the Kiskadee?" Lassiter asked casually.

"Tromped every inch of it, and took beaver out of every creek and pond. That was Blackfoot country when I first saw it, and they were still hell on all whites — let me be, though, account of I never did have a hair on my whole body, especially my head, which meant they couldn't count on me proper, not being able to lift my scalp."

He cackled in pleasurable remembrance — and sighed, adding, "Always wanted me a Blackfoot woman, but grabbing for one would have been a sure way to get myself killed, hair or no hair, since they didn't hold with that. Proud, haughty people; you'd think Effie had some of their blood in her, but she's all white."

Lassiter said, "Some caves up that way, along the Brule and the Kiskadee? — big caves, little caves — ?"

"Hell, no caves at all, that I know of, unless you'd count animal dens," Lonzo Moots replied.

"Old abandoned cabins, maybe a ghost town somewhere — ?"

"Nope. And no old abandoned mine, either, if you're thinking of asking that next. No gold ever showed in that country, placer or quartz. You want to get rich, head over west, to the new diggings; that's where the color is!"

Lassiter frowned. Some of that missing government money had shown up; if the rest was intact, it had to be kept somewhere, hidden, out of the fierce extremes of weather in this northwest country.

Somewhere in this town of Plumas, maybe — ? Lassiter was doubtful, though; it was perhaps only a hunch, but he felt it had not been moved very far, that it was still near the spot where Colonel Jason Follard supposedly had drowned.

He stirred, rising, bringing out a bill as he did so which he passed to Lonzo Moots. "Thanks for your help," Lassiter said. "Have a drink or two on me, sometime."

Scrambling to his feet, eyes glistening, the old man exclaimed, "Don't know what help I gave, but by Godfrey I'm sure pleasured by this cash seeing as how I'm drier than nine miles of badlands in August!"

Displaying astonishing speed for one of his years, he darted away, vanishing into darkness.

And Effie Moots shouted wrathfully, "Come back here, you weak-livered old whiskey guzzler!"

She appeared, running from the lean-to,

attired only in the knee-length drawers displayed on the boat. She had a charming boyish figure like shadowed ivory in the darkness, and her hair a loosely flowing jet mass about her shoulders. Darting after Moots, she fetched up at the fence, wheeled, came back.

"A week of watching him, down-river and back, to keep him sober; now, just when I dozed off for only a minute or two, you came along. He'll be drunk for a week!" she stormed. "God-damn you — !"

Lassiter reached out to squeeze a shoulder. "Ladies don't use such language," he said. "And you're still in need of that bath, smelling like a she-fox too long in the den — "

With a breathless cry, she made another earnest effort to claw his face. Lassiter caught and smothered her wind-milling arms. Jerking her off her feet with an arm about her slim waist, he carried her, kicking and yelling in a fury which made the mules mill uneasily, past the fire but not toward the lean-to. Instead, his destination was the water trough. Unceremoniously, he heaved her in.

She landed on her back with a resounding splash, sank under and came up with hair a sodden mass about her face, sputtering furiously. Her language was even more volcanic as she struggled to climb out of the trough.

Lassiter shoved her under again. "Stay put and soak for a while — and do it every day, after this!"

He left her with regret but with things to do. And to be done right away, the money wasted that he had laid out for a hotel room where he would not sleep tonight.

A hunch whispered urgently that Lonzo Moots had told him a lie. Lassiter was not certain what the lie was, or why it had been told, but he meant to find out as quickly as possible, leaving tonight, heading up-river.

Instead of going back through the pole fence to the dark alley where a stalker might lurk, he moved away from it, into a small barn, another livery stable, with a night lantern burning above its street door.

As he strode toward that lantern, Lassiter thought of something glimpsed from a corner of his eye at the moment of dropping half-naked Effie Moots into the watering trough. A keg of giant powder . . . part of the mule loads that Lonzo and the girl would be taking off to eastward — ? If so, why?

An alarm bell was ringing in him again. An instant later, he saw out on the street, by the lantern's light, a woman's figure and face. It was Amy Follard, peering toward him, fingertips fluttering to her lips in fright.

"No! Run!" she gasped before she faded back out of sight.

Somebody came at him, from inside the livery barn — he heard a hiss and snarl, and smelled the rank stench from last night . . .

Lassiter dropped flat to straw-littered, odorous ground. Then he lunged sideways, slammed into him shin-high as he raced to attack — made him howl, flung him sideways and down but only to bounce up with cat-like quickness, set to strike again.

Then someone else came lunging in from the street. The lantern light again showed a face. This one was scarred by old fights, skinned by recent ones, and Lassiter felt as though icy water had touched his spine.

It was Private Jay Suggs, neck broken last night, hurled into the black torrent of the Kiskadee, but alive again, coming fast, as though returning from his watery grave to strike anew at Lassiter — who, through a moment when inaction could be fatal, and well knowing this, still stood without moving as he tried to adjust to attack by a man who was certainly dead.

Suggs snarled obscenely and leaped at Lassiter, hands reaching to grip and tear. And the buck — the same one as last night? — was circling to strike at him from behind.

5

THEN the fellow who seemed to be Private Jay Suggs piled forcibly into Lassiter, and he was no ghost. He was very real and composed of hard muscle, bone and sinew, and he spit a string of malignant curses to accompany the explosion of his strength.

Perhaps only one factor prevented him from succeeding — the very fury of his assault. It was as though, hate burning in him like white heat, he wanted to rip Lassiter's head from his shoulders. At any rate, that's what he tried to do, snatching and twisting with both hands.

The stab of pain from that served to snap Lassiter out of his curious moment of lethargy. He jerked his head aside, had the full weight of the man against him for an instant with a driving force still in the press of his body.

Lassiter turned this to good account. With a sideward step, he clamped a hold on the other's body a little above waist high and he twisted, lifted him, and threw him — all in one swift flow of impressive strength.

It was adroit use of his antagonist's momentum, a trick of leverage he had mastered only after considerable practice.

Suggs howled in astonishment and dismay to discover he had lost his footing and was flying through the air. His cry was chopped off short as he slammed into the Indian, who was charging in a limp at Lassiter with a knife held low, no doubt to rip the softness of his belly from side to side. The knife flew away, the Indian was hurled flat, with Suggs piling on top of him, and for a moment they struggled, entangled, cursing frantically.

Lassiter drew his .44. "Now," he informed them, "you'll both get up, slow and easy, and stand right still . . . for straight answers to some questions, which you'll give fast when they're asked or I'll stick bullets in both of you, not meaning to kill but I guarantee you'll be feeling considerable hurt, of a kind to shrivel your maggoty souls — "

It was a good program for the immediate future, one which Lassiter meant to push to the limit, even if Suggs' eyes showed a wet, venomous sheen of hate. As for the Indian his eyes were like lava chips, with his lip curled to boast that he could withstand any pain.

The Indian was wrong; Lassiter could deal pain of a kind beyond their imagining. Both were going to talk.

Lassiter guessed that the Indian had somehow, improbably, swum out out of the Kiskadee last night ripped by Lassiter's bullet. While Suggs had not also escaped, verification of just who he was and where he fitted in was soon going to be forthcoming, or else.

Pointing his gun at Suggs, aiming low, Lassiter said, "You lead off. Talk — or I start by smashing your kneecaps — " But before he could speak Effie Moots came charging into the livery barn, uttering some wild, inarticulate cry, flourishing her Henry rifle, setting stock to shoulder and pulling trigger with an ear-squeezing roar.

She looked wild, also, and wholly improbable. She had not paused to dress. Her linen drawers, still wet and dripping, clung tightly to slender legs. Her uncovered skin had a glittering sheen. Dark hair straggled like hanks of soaked yarn about her face.

Lassiter, taken aback and a little slow in responding, gaped at her. It was a turn of events he could never have anticipated.

He was not much taken by her fetching display of skin; his first thought was to whip off his belt, turn her over his knee and make good use of the leather against her backside. But she yelled again, and with a quite competent flip of the rifle's cocking lever, pulled trigger again. Lassiter saw he must forget the other two and focus all of his attention on her, or he was quite liable to wind up shot.

Meanwhile, the men were on the move, trying a pell-mell rush for the door. Lassiter said, "Stay put, you rats!" and he snapped a bullet.

It was aimed at the Indian, as the one he most wanted in his hands, but the buck was zigging, jumping, and spinning like an Arapaho medicine man in the climactic moments of the Sun Dance, and the bullet was a miss.

Lassiter realized he had to let them go in order to do something about the rattler of a girl. She was whipping the cocking lever again. Her rifle held more than one lone cartridge tonight, and, left alone to continue firing, she was bound to score a hit.

So, in angry exasperation, he turned away from the two, now ramming and jostling each other in their haste to get through the street door. He had to cover about thirty feet of straw-littered ground to get his hands on her.

There was a wicked blaze in her eyes as she sighted the weapon, looking down its barrel at him, ready to blow his head off, if she could, fumbling at the trigger in an effort to pull it before his hands were on her.

A furious sweep of Lassiter's arm drove the weapon aside, slanting it upward. It roared a third time, and put a bullet-hole through a shake roof. He wrenched the Henry from her grasp and hurled it aside. She screamed and tried to bite him, tried again to rip his face with her long nails.

"You damned vixen, that's enough!" Lassiter said.

He whipped her aside. She landed hard, sitting down with legs spraddled, swearing. She stared up at him to see a blaze in his eyes also, and suddenly looked almost feminine as she shrank back a little and lifted her hands to cover her budding breasts.

For a second, Lassiter was tempted to haul her into one of the livery stalls, tear off her fancy drawers, and make her pay as women had been paying ever since Eve.

Then he shook his head; he had never

cared for immature females, and also he had other things to do. Time was now of the essence and pressing him hard.

Striding to the Henry, he scooped it up and worked its lever fast. Its brass glinted like sparks of fire and bullets flew, as he emptied the magazine. Empty, he threw it at her. She grabbed it, springing up, lip curling, very much the untamed vixen again.

Lassiter ran to the stable's street door. He was not greatly surprised to find the men gone. Amy Follard might possibly have lingered, at least, but she hadn't.

While he was making a quick check, a whiskery individual suddenly made a yawning appearance in the stable. It was the night hostler coming from an office or tack room at one side where he had a pallet or cot. He gawked at Effie in startled gratification, getting an eyeful.

With curled lip, she ran at him, crouched, swung the rifle's barrel, laid it against a shin with a brisk popping sound. It made him howl and dance on one foot, clutching at the hurt leg.

Lassiter shook his head at her termagant anger, hoping that luck, chance, or fate, would keep her out of his way from now on. He slid through the door and left. His last glimpse of Effie was of the girl down on her knees, scraping about in the dirt for her bullets, while the hostler continued to hop about in the background, moaning in pain.

Staying at the backs of buildings, Lassiter worked his way back along the street toward the other end of town. None of them were in sight, not Mungo, the woman, Suggs or the Indian. Not Stag Durkee. And he had no sense of being stalked.

At the other livery stable, where he had left the two horses bought earlier in the evening, he saddled the chestnut and put the pack gear on the bay. Then he rode out with the bay on lead, leaving by the rear.

Another night hostler had appeared, his expression plainly curious as to a customer's reason for leaving in the middle of the night and heading toward the black, almost trackless wilderness that began at the edge of town.

Lassiter tossed him a coin. It would no doubt take him to the nearest saloon to gossip about his curious behavior. Well, so be it; he had no illusions about covering his tracks for long. All he hoped to accomplish by leaving at this hour was to get the jump on Stag.

At first, no rider or riders came after him, but as he approached the dark sweep of forest that crowded close upon Plumas, a gun suddenly cracked behind him with the flat roar of a .45 and whine of lead somewhere close to his head.

The whine was followed instantly by the brassy blare of a laugh like a cracked and offkey bugle. Lassiter knew that laugh. Stag had checked Lassiter's moves and knew he was leaving town.

Lassiter, twisting in his saddle, pulled trigger also, firing at the sound of that laugh. A profane exclamation told him his bullet had missed.

Stag called, "You're still the quickest damned hand on the shoot I ever saw!

Hey, *compadre*, how about some palaver? Like I said in Denver, give me a piece of the action and a fair split, and I'll back you right up into Satan's front parlor!"

Lassiter reflected that if Old Nick ever should find Stag Durkee in his front parlor or any other part of his no doubt richly furnished palace area, it would be highly desirable to keep a close eye on hell's silver and other valuables.

"No dice then, Stag; no dice now! I never cottoned to running in double harness with anybody."

While speaking he was sliding out of saddle, just in case. It proved to be a savvy move, as Stag fired again with a gush of flame at about thirty yards. Lassiter knew the bullet had come quite close to where he had sat in saddle.

He did not make the mistake of thinking a bullet aimed at the source of gunfire might be profitable. There was no doubt that Stag, like himself, was on the move. Lassiter moved quietly off with the chestnut, working on toward forest cover, waiting, thinking it probable that

Stag would speak again. He was presently rewarded.

"Listen, *amigo*, you know I'll just keep coming on, and there's sure no profit in sight if we keep on bucking each other — "

Then Lassiter aimed at the sound of his voice. There was a sharp crack of the .44 and an abrupt chopping off of what Stag was saying. For a lengthening moment, Lassiter thought he might have scored a hit.

Then Stag spoke once more, now sounding somewhat sad and aggrieved, "I never thought it would come to this between you and me, and I'm right unhappy, *hermano*."

Lassiter snorted, wondering if Stag was also dripping crocodile tears. He was a man who could sit and smile while Lassiter was being burned alive, if there was profit in it for him. Stag had gone from comrade to friend to brother and Lassiter wasn't buying any of it.

At the edge of the trees there was the strong resinous scent of closely massed pines. Lassiter paused. He would not make the mistake of aiming still one more bullet at the sound of Stag's voice. He knew beyond doubt that the tough, canny gunman who was dueling with him had found good cover before speaking anew.

He was right. "I guess I'll just have to hang around this town and envy whatever you've come up with when you show again," he said. "But — hey! — how about sending Lurie to ride with you? She'll be a mighty nice comfort under your blankets!"

She would also probably be under orders to mark his trail, Lassiter thought. No, he decided. "*Hasta la vista*, Stag!"

Maybe he should have called, "*Hasta pronto!*" since Lassiter knew he and Stag would clash again, very soon.

6

WITH a good horse moving under him and sunlight hot against his back, Lassiter felt fine. Of all things he liked, this — a first rate mount, wild country and dim trails to follow — rated well up on the list.

Only, however, if there was some goal to be reached by such riding. And of course in this particular instance there was a goal and a fat prize to be won.

Or at least, Lassiter hoped so. Reviewing it all, especially last night, he got the same answer: he was heading in the best possible direction.

Somewhere before him, he was going to pick up the hot scent always given off by money in large quantity. He rated his chances somewhat better than even that he would find it, put his hands on the money, and head back down the Kiskadee with it in his possession.

He breathed deeply of the day's warm pine-scented air with the good feeling persisting. It did not dilute his pleasure that somebody was on his back trail.

He had anticipated being followed. It had begun a little sooner than he had anticipated, however. That meant somebody clever and ruthless was coming at him from behind.

Probably Stag Durkee, Lassiter guessed. He wondered if the burly, seam-faced hellion was coming after him alone or if that charmer with the red hair and snowy skin would be along also. If the latter was the case, Lassiter thought, Stag was quite likely to lose a girl. In fact, he might just turn back right now, and . . .

At this point, he felt a tightness between his shoulders. He tried to shake it off but could not do so; if anything it became even more pronounced. Lassiter saw it as a warning that somebody not Stag Durkee, was approaching from the rear.

He couldn't begin to comprehend how he knew this, and he did not greatly care.

All he did know was that something was telling him it was not Stag. What the something might be, warning him, didn't matter. What mattered was to heed the message that was being offered.

The time was well past the middle of the afternoon. He took stock of his position. He was on a fairly wide trail — too wide to be made by game, but possibly left as the mark of raiding Indian war parties. The Kiskadee was several hundred feet below at the base of a precipitate slope which fell almost straight down. On his left, another slope ran up and up, too steeply for even a mountain goat to climb. Lassiter was in one hell of a spot if anybody should suddenly come at him from either direction. It was highly desirable to get off this trail — preferably, not by making that long jump down to the turbulent river, which looked even more dangerous and deadly in this up-stream stretch.

The segment of trail he was on ran northward for half a mile or more before seeming to veer inland this side of a high, rounded rock formation which had the look of a skull. Lassiter spurred the chestnut gelding to a faster pace, which meant the bay had to move more briskly also. The bay was squealing and fighting its lead rope. Its empty pack-saddle jumped loosely, and its big splayed hoofs flopped about, kicking gravel in showers down to the river. Lassiter swore tensely, sure he was going to need both horses, not wanting to lose even the cranky bay in a fall from the trail.

He was sweating hard when he turned aside at the skull-shaped rock, and then turned again, leaving the trail, plunging into the thick forest.

Both horses protested now; they did not like the rough going in thick timber. Lassiter, who didn't care for it either, held them grimly to the course he had picked. He wanted them hidden, well out of sight, when whoever was following made that turn away from the river at the skull rock.

Looking about, he spotted a site that

might be as good as any — the upper end of a sizeable blowdown. Dismounting, Lassiter pulled and shoved at the two horses, working them into cover provided by jackdaw piles of dead trees and tangles of old brush.

He tied them there, quickly cut lengths from the lead rope and fashioned muzzles. There was no guarantee these would keep them quiet, but he had to leave the animals for a while and knew no other way to hold them silent.

Returning to the skull rock, Lassiter climbed it from the up-river side. His fingers and toes sought crannies and cracks. It was a chancy venture since it was slippery going, and also he had brought along the .30-.30. Just below the peak of its curving top, he flattened down with the rifle under him to make sure he would not be betrayed by sun-glint against steel.

It wasn't a great danger though, since experience had shown him people were remarkably obtuse when it came to such a simple matter as looking around every now and then for what or who might be in sight, particularly if they had to raise their eyes above eye level. Now, becoming immobile, he waited.

It seemed only a couple of minutes had passed when something came into sight. His lips pursed in a silent whistle as he counted them; first two, then four, and eight, finally nine in all.

A sizable band, and he did not have to do much guessing as to who they were, particularly since almost at once he sighted Amy Follard. She was fifth in the single file cavalcade, sitting saddle with some awkwardness in a singularly ugly long green skirt. But — where was Mungo?

Lassiter did not sight him or Suggs or anyone resembling an Indian buck.

The first two in line paused beside the skull rock, just after turning away from the river. They sat there, talking so close Lassiter could have spit on them.

They were a hard, tough-looking pair. "By God," one said, "this had better work! I've had a gutful and then some.

93

Pick and shovel work in those diggings until my back feels broke in at least three places."

"Yes," the other one agreed. "Staying low and waiting. Well, I'm fed up with both, a year of it now, every minute expecting maybe a hand on my shoulder and getting dragged off to some damned stockade, then twenty years or so at Leavenworth for deserting, since I couldn't buy my discharge, like you others . . ."

He leaned forward to peer at Amy Follard, approaching, then continued, "If that fancy piece still tries to hold out, I say strip her down and stretch her on a bed of hot coals. That should make her talk fast enough!"

"Hell, Kershaw, just strip her down and turn her over to me," the first one said. "I'll guarantee to squeeze out everything she ever knew . . . and do it quick, too!"

"I think we all ought to get turns on her, the trouble she's caused," the second man said. "I think I'll demand that, along with the twenty-five thousand that's my full share and that had damned well better be put in my hand — !"

They fell silent. The woman was riding past, her face set and still — lines at the corners of her mouth, Lassiter noticed, put there by either fatigue or fear.

The two men watched her as she made the turn past the rock and kept going. Then, shaking out their reins to move on again, the one called Kershaw had a final word, "Well, by this time tomorrow everything had better be settled, or else. This whole bunch looks like farmers heading for market in a peanut town. Put them in a column of twos and do some ass-kicking if necessary to make them smarten up and dress their line. Also, get them to a trot, or we'll be past dark getting to and across that damned ford — "

The last of them passed by. Lassiter waited, counting out five minutes in his head before he stirred, slowly rising, stretching to take the kinks out of cramped muscles.

95

As he did so, one of them suddenly appeared below him again, muttering, looking about on the ground. He had come back, probably seeking a lost piece of gear and, making the turn past the rock, swinging onto the trail above the river again, unaccountably he looked up before Lassiter could flatten down to hug the rock again.

Lassiter saw him clear-on horseback there below, youthful and tough-looking with a horse-like face and horse-like teeth yellowed by nicotine. The fellow sucked in air to scream a warning. In the same instant, he grabbed at a handgun, holstered at his hip.

Lassiter reacted instantly, leaping out and down, knowing the horse would probably move. It did snorting, trying to shy. He caught the rider shoulder-high with both boots, catapulting him from saddle. The man landed at the river side of the trail and over, dangling for a moment above the white-frothed rapids far below, clawing frenziedly to stop himself and then to climb back.

Lassiter landed hard also, but not quite at the trail's outer edge. From long practice he instinctively retained his balance and leaped instantly to strike again, .44 whipping out and forward, trying to catch the other man before he was fully on his feet. Any sound could bring the whole bunch pelting back.

His opponent was trying to draw with a handgun that swung up and out, its muzzle veering toward Lassiter who altered the swing of his own gun in mid-strike, slashed with the barrel of the .44, hammered a wrist-bone to knock the other gun away. Then Lassiter rammed the .44 barrel under the man's chin, forcing his head back.

Fingers clawed at punishing gun metal, then at Lassiter himself. Throat cruelly constricted, the man could not cry out, though his lips gaped wide. The two men stomped, slid and slipped in a narrow circle at the very edge of the steep drop-off. Eternity was certain if they went over. Thick yellow dust rose about them in a stifling cloud, and the river sang its wild song far below.

His features rigid as though graven in stone, Lassiter saw he was caught in a dilemma. He had to maintain pressure on the gun, since letting up could mean an out-cry.

He did not dare let up to try for a quick skulling of the man, or to back away from that deadly drop-off, for any slip might send him over the edge.

It came to him, however, that faking a move might serve as well as the move itself, so he let up abruptly, with a half step back and away, though still holding the gun against the man's throat. The fellow stumbled toward him. Lassiter dropped his .44, shifted his hands fast, gripping the man's belt near the buckle. Then, turning, he thew the man over his hip.

The man was heavy, and might well have pulled Lassiter with him, but he hurtled out and away into the thinness of that void several hundred feet deep.

Swaying, arms windmilling, Lassiter somehow managed to keep his footing.

He watched the man fall.

There was a cry, thin and eerie like the distant *skree*! of a hawk. Then water splashed far below. The man had vanished, and he would not re-appear.

Lassiter slowly bent to pick up the .44. He looked around for the other's gun, and kicked it into the river after him. His horse was gone, frightened and running back along the trail. Let it run, Lassiter thought, away from those others.

Walking back to his own two horses, he thought fast. He would follow along, spot that ford across the Kiskadee as it was being used, cross to the other side after them, again follow along, get close . . .

And, he asked himself, what then — ?

There was a good reason to tag after that bunch. They would lead him to the money as she was leading them. Amy Follard was the key. She knew where the money was hidden but had not yet revealed this information to anyone.

She would reveal it to him, Lassiter resolved, when he took her away from those others. He did mean to take her away from them and had every confidence in his ability to do so.

His smile widened as he thought of Amy Follard. He was remembering the night when she had shared the narrow berth with him in the stateroom of a rickety river boat.

Mounting up, he moved through timber at a driving pace, close to the trail, following the group. He was in a hurry to grab Amy and get the information he needed.

7

LASSITER was prone, belly down, almost buried in a pile of dead leaves, pine needles and assorted wind-blown brush. He was keeping watch on a fire in a small clearing perhaps a hundred feet away.

It was a fire set at a spot picked for a night camp, and was considerably larger than needed. An Indian or skilled woodsman could make do with a blaze that could be contained in a man's hat. Those yonder obviously had a craving for plenty of fire and its light at this gray moment of dusk when full night was only moments away.

Amy Follard sat on a rock, facing toward the fire. She was turned sideways toward Lassiter. Her head was lowered and all the lines of her figure spoke eloquently of weariness and perhaps fear. Her green skirt was damp and muddy.

A youthful, lean, lantern-jawed man faced her with a rifle under one arm. "Sweetie, you and me might as well get along," he said. "I got orders to stay right with you, anywhere you go . . . and I do mean anywhere!"

He sniggered. The woman did not respond or look up.

The debris which almost hid Lassiter stirred slightly, with the faintest of rustling sounds, as he began to inch forward. He had to get closer, close enough to whip the .44's barrel against the back of the rifleman's neck. But, before that, he had to learn if others were on the prowl, and if so, where.

Tracking down this bunch, after crossing the Kiskadee, had been no very demanding feat. The water ran fast and shallow over a rock ledge maybe thirty feet long. Lassiter had given them a lead of a good half hour before fording it. Then he had worked slowly across, taking his time. The bay had presented his only problem. The fractious spooked animal fought him constantly, but he had gotten both animals across and quickly into cover while he looked for tracks.

He found them. The riders were bearing almost due north, close to the river and along another ancient dim trail threading through thick stands of lodgepole pine and spruce. Lassiter had followed at a slow pace.

Lassiter remembered the final talk at the skull rock. One of them had fretfully demanded a military formation and bearing. This could mean skirmishers were around. Somebody might be riding behind as rear guard. If so, Lassiter had no particular desire to barge into that somebody.

If there were such a rider, however, he didn't meet him. When he saw a camp fire through many rows of trees, he had stopped, made a tie of his horses in thick cover and worked toward that fire. He approached on a long, elliptical route meaning to come at them from the north on the principle that they might be least wary of possible attack from that direction.

Keeping his head down so he would not be betrayed by firelight finding the glitter of his eyes, Lassiter continued his approach, .44 in his fist. The only plan he had was to get within rushing distance undetected, then to run at the fellow with the rifle, dispose of him fast, and grab for the woman. But he was bothered by the fact that he could not spot any of them.

Some minutes ago there had been several of them in view, moving about beyond the fire where the horses were probably tethered. Now all that could be glimpsed during the swift looks that he risked were two: the lanky lantern-jawed fellow with the rifle slanting down under his arm and Amy Follard.

The man was speaking again. "Golly, all the times I saw you there, at that damned Fort Furlong, you the high and mighty Colonel's wife, no more heed for me, a rear-rank private, than if I was a damned worm — and me wanting so bad I could taste it to put my hands on you just once — like this — "

Bending, a loose, writhing grin on his long face, he reached to the woman and seized and held a breast through the rumpled cloth of a thin blouse.

Gasping, she tried to shrink back from him while attempting to break his grip. He held on, his smile widening, becoming a wheedling smirk. "Ah, don't play hard to get with me! You're no better than any pay-day whore; I've seen it plenty of times in your eyes — like today, sizing all of us up, ready to cozy under the blankets of anybody who'd help you get away — !"

Lassiter began the count in his head for the moment, only seconds away, when he would leap to his feet, drive at that dirty-mouth man who was so greedy with his fondling he'd forgotten the necessity to be on guard in all directions.

It was not the despoiling of Amy Follard that was prompting him to act. The swift onset of darkness offered him the opportunity, and darkness would shield them both when he began to run with her, plunging her into the deep timber. Given a head start of a hundred feet or so, he was willing to bet they would never be overtaken.

He paused, however, looking still for the others, a precaution that just might have saved his life. From behind him a heavy footstep suddenly sounded, and a man's deep voice called commandingly, "Kershaw!"

Lassiter froze, head down on folded arm, but watching from under the brim of his hat.

He saw men move beyond the fire; he counted three of them, all with rifles at the ready, glancing this way with arms raised in salutation, then fading back from sight again.

Another man showed yonder, coming at a hurried stride, passing the fire with a hard side glance for the fellow who was guarding Amy Follard, who was now standing and looking somewhat confused. This newcomer was the one called Kershaw who had issued the orders about military formation and bearing by the skull rock. "What in the hell is going on here?" he snapped. "Get away from her, stand at attention as a sentry should, and keep your eyes peeled. Damn your hide, do it!"

The man came on, responding to a newcomer's call. He tramped past Lassiter at a distance of about a dozen feet, without noticing a half-buried log in a drift of leaves By the fire, the other one glared angrily, but he made a show of alertness, facing away from Lassiter. The woman, grimacing, touched herself at the bosom, and wearily began to smooth her rumpled blouse. Her attitude was one of hopelessness and bitterness.

Behind Lassiter, Kershaw spoke, "By God, I was riding a razor, afraid something had happened and you wouldn't show!"

The deep-voiced man growled, "You're like a woman, with your worries. And, speaking of women — ?"

Lassiter sensed the two were looking toward Amy Follard, and that she was looking toward them with a sudden stillness and stiffness in her attitude.

Kershaw said, "Well, she hasn't done

any talking yet. I've had a tough time of it, keeping this bunch of studs away from her. They're all on fire to grab hold and turn her every way but loose."

A deep voice said, "Pass the word that it will go hard with any man who touches her before I squeeze her for what she's going to tell. After that, they can have her, turn and turn about — "

The two men walked toward the fire, again quite close to Lassiter but without glancing his way. Motionless, he had the .44 beside his cheek, hammer eared back. Let them see him — they were both dead men. At this distance he couldn't miss.

Then the two did pause, but with their backs toward Lassiter. Kershaw said, "We're missing a man — Odem. He turned back, before we hit the ford. He had a double eagle, his lucky piece, hung on a leather whang around his hat brim. He said that he suddenly noticed the whang was worn through and the coin gone, but maybe he could find it. I didn't know all that till he was gone. I'll have him stripped and whip some blood out of him with my quirt when he shows, for disobeying orders that nobody turns back."

"No. You'll shoot him," the other man growled. "Though maybe he won't be along. We've got one party, at least, somewhere on our back trail. Maybe two parties. Odem could have quit, throwing in with one of those others."

"Jesus!" Kershaw muttered. "If we've waited so goddam long, gone through so much, only to get aced out now — !"

The head of the other man turned, showing a bushy beard in profile.

"We aren't going to be aced out," the deep voice said. "Tomorrow or the next day, no later, we wind it all up. By God, we will!"

"Amen to that," Kershaw muttered. "The longest damned year anybody ever had to live through . . . because of a woman! Listen, give me first turn at her when you toss that conniving bitch to us !"

Then somebody passed Lassiter with a weasel-like rush. He smelled the Indian stench again; it was angling toward the fire and then away from it.

Kershaw and the bearded man — Mungo, Lassiter supposed — were going on, with some talk of checking sentries and horses, then of eating. They, too, angled away from the fire. The move took them away from the woman without a word to her.

Lassiter, stirring, listening, looking in all directions, knew it was time. "Now!" he told himself.

Nothing was to be gained by more waiting. Only Amy Follard and the man guarding her were in sight. Lassiter surged to his feet.

He stood for a moment, lips tight, .44 in his fist. He was measuring time and space, taking his bearings.

The prospect looked promising. The guard was at the woman again, bending to fondle her, grinning as he rammed a hand into the neckline of her blouse.

Lassiter moved fast. With luck, he'd put the fellow into black oblivion before he knew he'd been hit.

But Lassiter did not rely on luck. He was not fazed when the man abruptly straightened and wheeled toward him. Some whisper of sound — or instinct — had warned him. In panic, he tried to swing his rifle at the dark figure rushing at him.

Lassiter had included this counter-move in his calculations. With a twist of a sinewy wrist he rammed the butt-plate of his gun hard against the man's chin.

Craacck! The man's rifle flew from his nerveless fingers. He fell back two steps, as his legs were caving in under him, then he lay still, staring senselessly up at the stars.

He might have to drink all of his meals until his cracked jaw healed, Lassiter thought, but he was better off than the one named Odem.

He warned the woman with gun muzzle to lips, to be quiet. She was staring at him as at an apparition.

But the warning was effort wasted. A hoarse voice blared a warning, "Somebody at the fire! He just skulled Malloy!"

A handgun roared with two fast shots. There was another yell and the spiteful crack of a rifle. A tree branch fell near Lassiter's face.

Holding his own fire for the moment, he reached for the woman's hand and jerked her up to her feet. For a second, with a wordless keening of protest, she struggled, eyes wide, breath short with fear.

"You want to stay, and let each of them take his turn on you? Move!" Lassiter ordered.

He spun her around. Stumbling, she went in the direction he indicated — toward the river. Lassiter followed, only pausing to fire a fast round of bullets, aimed in a spread, left to right. Somebody yelped in pain. Shadowy converging figures hit the ground for a moment. Lassiter ran on, though all of them must now know the direction he was taking.

Ramming fresh shells into the .44 as he moved, he bumped against Amy Follard. She was already gasping in fatigue.

Somebody was coming at them from the right, yelling, "What in the hell?"

Lassiter had anticipated a sentry would be posted somewhere in that direction. Back toward the fire, Kershaw shouted obscenities, adding, "Coming right at you; stop him!"

Lassiter pulled the woman down. He crouched beside her, waiting. The sentry came on and might have passed by but he spun suddenly at them and opened up, gunfire crashing, gunflame winking. He was yelling again, ferociously, but it all ended abruptly as Lassiter came up beside him with a fast, deft feathering of gun barrel at his neck.

The man hit the ground. Lassiter grabbed Amy Follard again and shoved her forward. The roar of the river was loud before them. She gasped anew, staggering cramped by her skirt. He paused to rip it with both hands. He peeled it off and started her running once more. They made an abrupt turn to the south, alongside the river rather than toward it.

Lassiter was gambling that he could find his way through thick timber and primordial blackness better than the pursuers. All of his senses were honed to extra sharpness.

They were making a great deal of racket behind him, shouting constantly as they crashed through thick underbrush. Several torches were bobbing about. Lassiter paused a moment to line on one of those blossoms of fire and was rewarded. A dark figure cut in front of it, coming straight at him.

He forced the woman down again and crouched beside her. He was picking up moccasin whispers that echoed against forest sluff. He surged up, with a swing of a gun-weighted fist, catching the other in the gut. Leathery muscles resisted but gave way, and sour-smelling air hit his face as the buck snapped down like a closing jackknife. He sprawled kicking and wheezing for breath.

Lassiter ran on, hauling the woman along, rather regretting he couldn't risk betrayal of his position by use of a bullet to put that one out of the way for good. He was confident now they would make it to his two horses. After that, in a night camp somewhere, well hidden Amy Follard would talk.

His small fire snapped softly. There was a coffee pot steaming, and the horses shuffled about. A wolf was howling off a couple of miles.

Lassiter had chosen a fairly deep ravine with precipitate side walls of rock. The horses were up-canyon. A screening of brush lay below. He felt confident no one would spot this place.

Amy Follard sat near the fire. Her head was bent and her fingers were picking at a thin, brief underskirt. Lassiter noted again the superb tapering of her legs.

When she spoke her voice was thin, desolate, but firm. "I wouldn't tell them, not ever. I won't tell you, either."

Her head lifted. Warming his hand on a tin cup of coffee, Lassiter saw bitterness in her eyes. "That money is mine, all mine. I earned it in the years

115

I had to spend as Follard's wife."

She made a dreary, lip-tightening grimace. "If I can't have it — nobody can! And I wanted you to kill for me. I ask it again. I was ready to die, when I was with them. I am quite as ready now. So kill me! Give me a bullet, quickly . . ."

She plucked at her blouse, tore it, beginning to uncover herself. "Do it, or I will begin to scream and keep on screaming. I kept track; they are not so far away, and they will hear. So shoot me. Not my face, though — at my heart. One bullet — then you can leave me here. Oh, God, use your gun, before I start to scream anyway! I can't stand living any longer!"

8

LASSITER stared at Amy Follard. Her breast was uncovered and beautiful and she was pleading that he shatter it with a bullet. He snorted, shattering instead the web of tension she had woven.

"*Bastante*, woman! Enough of this talk about killing — and screaming. And it isn't your money — but that isn't to say you can't have a fat chunk of it for yourself, since I'll split with you what I'm going to make from finding and turning it in. Fifty-fifty, down the line . . . including the cash from the Indian trading posts — "

Letting the effect of this sink in, he took a deliberate swallow from his cup. "And how much we keep of that trading post money depends on whether the numbers of the bills were written down, as with the Army cash. Were they?"

"No!" The word burst from her. He saw her eyes flicker as though in hurried, confused thought.

"We'll dicker a reward for returning it, then — half of the full amount. It will be paid, since whoever is legally entitled to it will know they are liable to wind up with nothing, inasmuch as otherwise the full amount might be spent by the finders, us, without detection. You'll get half of that reward. The government is offering me twenty percent for coming up with the Army money; I'll give you half of that, also."

She was now staring at him, lips parted, no longer thinned in bitterness, and it was obvious she had forgotten her talk about dying. "You're lying to me!" she said, but her tone was uncertain. Lassiter snorted again. "You've dealt too much with men who meant to squeeze you, use you, then throw you aside like a piece of trash. I don't deal in lies. And I do pay an honest price to everybody who helps me. Lead me to that money and you'll never regret it!"

She seemed to ponder it. Lassiter walked toward the horses. They were pegged up-canyon and he was vaguely bothered by their muttering and shuffling, even though the wolf had howled again and that was seemingly reason enough for their restlessness.

But before he reached the horses he turned about, walking back toward Amy with the first of some carefully planned questions. "That Army ambulance was swept away at the ford where the Brule and the Kiskadee meet, but the money wasn't in it . . . right?"

She gave him a brief stare and a jerky nod, yes.

He pushed on, "It had been taken from the ambulance and hidden somewhere close to that ford. Quite close, I think, a place out of the weather, not easy to find — and known only to you. Whereabouts? What spot did you pick, before the ambulance was driven on and wrecked at the ford? That was to set up the story that the money was lost in the river, wasn't it?"

She didn't deny it but didn't add anything, either. Her gaze flickered about the small camp where shadows came and went like writhing demons. It was as though she was looking for some sign that would tell her what to do.

"Get something straight," Lassiter said, "because nothing is going to change it. You have no chance — none! — to grab the cash and get away with it alone. The only chance you do have is to work with me. So can we start now and make it there ahead of those others?"

Her lips fluttered. Lassiter added, "Working together, we can grab it, and clear out. Your share, free and clear, will run thirty thousand at least — more likely, forty, and possibly even more — "

Just as she was about to speak Amy cried out in fright and tried to scramble up and away.

Lassiter started to spin about, hand flashing to his .44. But a gun muzzle gouged his back. Stag Durkee said, "Easy, *muchacho*! You don't stand a chance. Hands out, wide. Do it!"

Angry, Lassiter obeyed. At once, he saw how it had happened, Stag, working up-canyon, had come at him from that direction. Stag was one of the few men alive, in Lassiter's opinion, who could accomplish that. He was the one, of course, who had almost spooked the horses — but Stag, who could calm a savage dog, had kept them quiet enough so they hadn't quite revealed him.

Stag had won this round. Lassiter had been too involved with Amy Follard. Well, he had once heard Stag characterized as somebody who could wiggle buck-naked through forty acres of cactus and not be fanged by a single spine. Now, Lassiter's hands went out slowly to his sides, as ordered.

Lurie now appeared, coming from down-canyon, pert in levis, wool shirt, and boots. Her hair was like flame by firelight. She murmured something to Amy, gesturing her to move back toward the fire. Her glance touched Lassiter and flicked swiftly away.

Lassiter was in iron control of himself

again, "'*Sta bien*, Stag. Call it, *hombre*. You're holding high card."

"*Seguramente*. Turn around," Stag ordered. "Do it slow!"

Lassiter turned to face the burly, seam-faced man. His eyes were snapping foxily. Stag held a .45 on him the way it should be held — a little forward, just above belt level, elbow against body, the gun as still as death. Stag had backed off fast to obviate any attempt by Lassiter to spin about, drive the gun up, and grapple him.

"I've got all the aces, right here in my fist," Stag said. "As you damned well know."

Lassiter nodded in recognition of the obvious. To try for his .44 would be absolute suicide, one hundred times out of one hundred. Stag ranked with the very best, ranked with Lassiter himself. Fate might intervene to alter the odds, Lassiter thought, but it was not likely Stag would alter them through some blunder.

"Got quite an earful of your gab with

that woman, and I'll give you high credit — as usual with those you pick, she's *muy hermosa*," Stag said, with an appreciative glance at Amy Follard. "So I know all about it — your game and what you're playing for. Not that I needed to do much guessing, coming up-river and hearing those stories about the government cash that was lost. It's just the kind of game that would hook you . . . and me."

He grinned, in tigerish amiability. "Somewhere near here, and hidden, with only the lady knowing where — ? Well, I'll just have to take her over, do some squeezing and pocket that big bundle of cash. All of it. Sorry like hell, but you wouldn't cut me in back at Denver, and I'm not cutting you in now."

Stag would never have cut Lassiter in, either; there was no way any deal could be set up between them. Stag meant to take everything. Lassiter knew, too, that Stag did not intend he should leave here alive.

This meant Stag must be tackled, no

matter the degree of peril in such a move. All possible moves flashed through Lassiter's head — at high speed, for Stag was not a man to spend much time in talk.

A direct attack would probably be the best of his forlorn chances, Lassiter decided. He would attempt to close his fingers on Stag's throat. He must stop a bullet; it was impossible for Stag to miss at such close range. He could only hope that by twisting, turning, and narrowing the target offered for Stag's .45, he might evade a mortal wound.

Then, bracing himself for attack and possibly suicide, Lassiter noticed that Lurie was up to something.

Lurie had moved toward the fire, but had worked on past it, idling on up-canyon a little. Her gaze was fixed in an almost painfully intense manner on Stag Durkee until she was behind him. Suddenly she produced a small handgun from under her skirt, jabbed Stag in the back with its muzzle as he had jabbed Lassiter, then stepped as quickly away.

Taken wholly by surprise, Stag seemed to shiver a little, though he kept his attention riveted on Lassiter.

"Drop it, Stag," Lurie said, her voice ragged. "If you don't, I'll have to shoot you, and then I'll want to die, too, but I swear I'll shoot you."

"Girl, you've gone loco," Stag said. "Put your pop-gun away. I won't belt you for pulling it on me; you've got my word I won't."

"You promised me that you wouldn't hurt him," Lurie said.

"And I won't. A bullet in the heart doesn't hurt. He'll never know it happened."

"I can't let you do it, Stag," the girl said, tears in her voice. "I just can't!"

"Oh, Christ!" Stag Durkee said. "Why in the hell couldn't you have been just another empty-headed bitch out of Mrs. Fike's stable of tarts, ready to do anything you're told for a few dollars?"

He was a man cruelly squeezed in a vise. He didn't dare turn to Lurie. Lassiter would draw instantly and kill him if he did. If he shot Lassiter a bullet from Lurie's gun would be smashing into him.

Nevertheless, an abrupt change in his bearing warned that he meant to make this latter move. His eyes narrowed to pinpoints, and Lassiter saw in them a steely resolve. Only someone of Stag Durkee's calibre was capable of such resolve.

"Last chance, Lurie," Stag said. "I'll get him, and then I'll get you. That's only a .25 you're holding; you'll have to score dead center to stop me with it, and I don't think you can do that. So either you be the one to drop a gun and come around here where I can see you, or else. And I'll hate to shoot a woman, never did that yet, but I won't hesitate a second if you don't move quick — "

She was interrupted by Amy Follard, forgotten in the background. Amy slammed into high brush, down-canyon, and thrashed through that, with high cry, thin, fearful, and still another, carrying far in the quiet night.

Stag Durkee's eyes shifted just slightly, his attention veering.

Lassiter took the chance. He went at Stag, knowing every move he made must be certain.

The .45 whipped up at him with slash of crimson flame and a spot of blue at its heart. The explosion crashed deafeningly in Lassiter's ears, and burning powder seared his cheek. He seized the gun-wrist and forced it up. Then his other hand was at Stag's throat — and closing with a grip like an iron claw.

Rammed close together, chest to chest, they vied for an instant in a fierce contest of power. Stag Durkee was using his weight advantage to bear Lassiter down. Lassiter opposed this with an explosion of the raw-hide strength.

At the same time, he felt threat of Lurie with her gun. He had to swing Durkee, to use him as a shield and end this fight quickly, before Lurie shifted her position and shot him to save Stag.

Stag pistoned knees and heels at Lassiter, clawed at his throttling hand, then at his face, and tried ferociously to butt him. Stag was a man who had never granted quarter in his life — or asked it. He knew only one way to fight — to the death. The glare of his eyes, bulging in strain, the distorted writhing of his lips, said that was how this battle must end.

Lassiter knew it and mustered all of his resources to make certain he was not the one who died here. He had to shake the gun out of Stag's fist, then had to batter the man down with such ferocity that he could not rise again — and he must do these things in only a space of seconds.

They stamped close to the burning fire and with a twist of his wrist Lassiter knocked the .45 aside, and then rammed his fist deeply into Stag's middle.

There was no softness under Lassiter's knuckles; Stag Durkee had not let himself go to fat. Nevertheless, the blow seemed to have effect, as Stag moaned and shuddered.

Lassiter followed up with a very fast blow to the head, his fist sledging toward the temple. Like a suddenly emptied bag, the man whom Lassiter had thought as tough as a grizzly sagged against him, sliding downward.

Releasing his throttling throat-hold, Lassiter stepped back. He saw Stag fall to his knees and huddle there, head bent, pawing at it with both hands, his whole body shaking.

Then Stag looked up at him with a painful twist and lift of his head. His eyes showed dull resignation. "So give me a bullet, damn it," he said, voice hoarse. "Because that's exactly what I would do if I stood in your boots."

"Don't tempt me," Lassiter growled. "What in the hell, Stag?"

Lurie came scurrying over and dropped to her knees, both arms about Stag, pulling his head against her bosom. "It's the pain in his skull," she informed Lassiter. "Sometimes it nearly drives him mad."

She crooned softly as a mother to a child.

Lassiter chewed at his lip, chafed by

the number of people who had begged him lately to shoot them.

Logic advised that he should oblige Stag Durkee. Sparing him could mean he might again trail Lassiter, but for several reasons Lassiter decided against it.

For one, he suddenly had a powerful hunch as to just what the lie was that Lonzo Moots had told him and a further strong hunch as to exactly where to look for the hidden money. Lassiter bet he would have his hands on it before night.

If so, there was no need to deal Stag Durkee out. Let him live to savor the fact he had locked horns with Lassiter and had wound up decidedly second best. Let him find out Lassiter had all of the money and was gone with it.

Beginning to move toward his horses, Lassiter spoke to Lurie, "Girl, look after him. Get him back to Plumas, and have a doctor check his head."

Stag said hotly, "I'm coming right after you — and I'll get you, too, the very next time we meet!"

Lassiter heard no further sound from Amy Follard. He wondered if the bunch by the river had grabbed her again.

He said to Stag Durkee, "Aim real good, if we ever do meet again — and make sure your first bullet kills. Because I'll see to it you don't live to fire a second shot."

9

BY the close of the following afternoon, Lassiter discovered one of his hunches had been correct. He was near the spot where the Brule and Kiskadee Rivers met.

His other hunch, however, had been wrong. The money was not there.

It had been a hot, humid day, with thunderstorms crashing and cannonading all about the high, lonely country. Both Lassiter and his horses were uncomfortable.

He had had a look at the brawling uproar of water where the wild rivers poured together, then had moved on beside the Brule, until he spotted the ford where the Army ambulance had tried to cross. That river there flowed over another rock ledge that was only about thirty yards wide and maybe twice as long, but the current there was no more than hub-deep on a wheeled rig.

It was difficult to see how any reasonably competent driver could manage to let the current sweep an ambulance into a mile or more of rapids to southward. It confirmed Lassiter's suspicion that the ambulance had been deliberately wrecked and lost.

He felt also that the man who had died in that accident — if anyone had — must have been already dead when it happened.

Easily crossing, Lassiter looked for and soon spotted an old wagon road, weed-grown and not much used. The road was the reason that the ambulance had crossed at that ford. Sharply watching for another road, he still almost missed it. The set of wheel-tracks branched northwestward, almost obliterated by second-growth timber and high dead brush from last summer.

Following this branch road, which meandered at random and twice seemed to stop at dead-ends, only to appear again farther on, Lassiter rode for five miles or more, before something loomed through the timber ahead.

It was what he had expected to find somewhere near the junction of those two rivers; the skeletal housing for pulleys, ropes and the like above the shaft of an old mine, near the crest of a steep up-slope. For a fair bet, it was a memento of the first gold rush into this country, which had soon petered out, back in '68.

Working up to the long-abandoned, weathered beams, Lassiter saw at a glance he'd gained nothing in particular. The shaft was choked with timbers, large rocks, and dirt, and a spread of thick vegetation said it all had been in place a long while.

"Damn!" Lassiter said.

Glancing about, he glimpsed several buildings — a barn that was falling down, several sheds, and a house of cut timber that was a burned-out shell.

Five minutes were enough to prove there was no spot in any of those structures which could serve as a hiding place or had done so recently.

He stood in frustration for a moment, wondering if he had figured everything all wrong. A review of the facts said no. Logic insisted the money had to be here and in all likelihood close enough to reach within moments.

Putting his horses in cover at a thick motte of young alders about fifty yards from the mine shaft, Lassiter retraced his steps, and with the shaft as a central point began to move in a widening circle, studying every inch of ground with sharp, probing intentness.

Meanwhile, he found himself thinking of Amy Follard.

He had tried to find her last night in the darkness, and had failed. She must have found some place to hide without making any sound whatever. He had heard Mungo and his bunch thrashing through timber in search for the woman, and coming closer than Lassiter liked.

At last, he had decided to ride on, keeping riding through the night, and get a jump on them. Now that jump was being dissipated, as his search continued with no result.

Upwards of an hour of hunting failed to turn up anything but several mounds of what looked like freshly turned earth less than a month old along the base of a rocky ridge north of the mine shaft.

"Could the stuff just have been hidden in the ground, then dug up again — ?" Lassiter muttered.

But the number of those holes and their distances from each other argued against this possibility.

He felt a sense of chafing and exasperation. Returning to his horses, in cover among the alders, he stood, dourly considering whether to let the whole thing go and haul out — or wait for Mungo and his followers to arrive, though this presupposed they would have grabbed Amy Follard and at last had persuaded her to talk.

Then, suddenly, he saw something.

It was an opening under a heavy square boulder — a grizzly's winter den, it seemed, not an uncommon sight in this northwestern country. It was not the opening itself that caught Lassiter's attention. He saw a flick of color against the boulder.

He went to kneel and touch it, a bit of cloth wedged into a rock crevice. The cloth was a dark shade of red, and, rubbed between his fingers, it had the feel of silk.

The opening beneath the boulder was small, but large enough for a woman to squeeze herself down through it — and for a lean, rangy man, cramping himself somewhat, to do the same.

With a sense of growing excitement, Lassiter made hurried preparations, looking about for a chunk of wood to use as a torch, then lifting a coil of rope from his saddlehorn. At last he went to the opening under the boulder and began to work himself into it, feet first.

For a high odds bet, a woman had preceded him into the ground here — Amy Follard, leaving a marker torn from her attire. How she had ever learned of this place . . . but never mind;

right now the only information Lassiter wanted was the exact location of that money.

Lassiter slid into the fissure at an easy angle for twenty feet or so, then into a drift almost high enough for him to stand erect, running off, and slightly downward, toward the mine shaft.

There was no need for the rope to guide him back, since there seemed to be only this one underground drift, nor was there much need of the torch, inasmuch as small overhead crevices admitted spears of light.

Lassiter worked along the drift, hunched down, with a smell of dust and of years of decay in his nostrils. He thought of the arduous labor put out long ago to dig this tunnel.

There were stretches where he could see with good clarity, then dark stretches, where the light filtering through those crevices in rock overhead did not reach. But, working along, he began to feel dubious about the whole thing.

Lassiter never down-rated anyone — but

it seemed highly unlikely Mungo and company had not located this drift and investigated it also. They obviously had not found anything; it seemed unlikely he would, either.

Still, nagging at him was the fact that the woman must have come underground here. For what purpose, if not to hide the money — ?

The drift ended at a tangle of crushed timbers and heaped-up boulders, probably at or near the mine shaft. Glancing at that debris, Lassiter saw a dull glint of metal. He picked up some sort of pry bar, a thin length of tooled iron, and he stood holding this, trying to figure why it had been brought into the tunnel, and when.

Presently he faced about and started back, now feeling both sides of the drift, fingers testing the walls. No more than about thirty feet from where the tunnel ended, he discovered what appeared to be a seam.

It was in a dark section of the tunnel. He fingered the vertical break in the rock wall. There was a horizontal seam joining it about head-high.

Thumping the wall at that spot he heard a sound of wood rather than rock, so he inserted the edge of the pry bar into the vertical seam and put his weight against it.

With a groaning, creaking sound, a narrow, thick-beamed door set flush with the rock came slowly open. He lit a match. The sulphurous spurt of flame revealed a narrow, fairly deep room that opened off the drift, perhaps once intended for storage of explosives. Now the room held two suitcase-size leather satchels, plus a third that was somewhat smaller.

It took only a moment to open them up. Two of the satchels were crammed with fat blocks of bills ranging in size from five to a hundred dollars. Each block circled by a paper band with an inked notation of the total amount in the block, uniformly one thousand dollars. They were all new bills, mint-fresh — the Army money.

The third satchel held more blocks of cash, but older bills, tied about with twine. This, it seemed, was the money sent along from the Indian trading posts.

Amy Follard had known of this tunnel, and of that door, or her husband had, and Mungo had not known, had no doubt hunted here but without success. Mungo was likely due again, and it behooved Lassiter not to be caught here.

Leaving the door standing open, with no time available to shove it closed again, he worked at his best speed, carrying the three satchels out of the tunnel with his .44 gripped in his right fist.

Hastily, he wriggled back through the opening under the boulder, shoving the satchels ahead of him. After that, it required only a scant handful of minutes to put them in the packsaddle on the bay, and he was ready to go.

His thoughts leaped ahead. He could make it back across the Brule before dark, push on, cover miles southward this night; he could be in Plumas again two days from now, either to return down the Kiskadee on Cap'n Strunk's ramshackle boat or to ride the river trails in the same direction.

Either way, by mid-week or a little later, he should be handing over the Army cash to Anson Brett at LeGrande, reserving to himself the dickering for the return of the money from the Indian posts.

It did not rest very well that Amy Follard was not here to claim the share he had promised, and to be properly grateful to him. But, damn it, time taken for a quixotic hunting of her could be disastrous.

Then Lassiter heard voices. He moved alertly to the edge of the alders for a look, and said, "Oh, hell — no!"

He had sighted a ramshackle wagon with unsteady wheels and a dirty canvas tilt, drawn by a pair of rawboned, baleful-eyed mules. Lonzo Moots was handling the rig's reins. Effie was scrambling down from beside him.

Lonzo sighted Lassiter first, and gave an agitated, protesting yelp. "Hey, now, you don't belong here, so get out, right now! It's our place, we filed for it, legal and proper, after I found the color that those mush-heads who worked it years ago never did turn up, spite of all their fancy digging — "

This explained the holes and the piles of dirt along the base of that spiny ridge. They were exploration holes, the tracing of what Lonzo Moots had fancied to be a vein of gold-bearing ore.

The day's light was dimming and black clouds bellied low. Lightning flickered; thunder cracked sharply.

Lassiter sent a glance at Effie Moots. She seemed unaccountably quiet. She gripped her rifle with one hand and was using the other to tug down a brief skirt in an effort to hide her bare legs. A flow of color showed in her cheeks.

Strange as it seemed, Effie was embarrassed — for the moment, at least — in Lassiter's presence.

He turned back to Lonzo. "Have done

with your squawking, old man. I'm not interested in your prospect holes, or the mine you said wasn't here. Dig all you damned please!"

It seemed obvious Lonzo had told more than one lie, that he and the girl headed here fast for the purpose of working a claim that they were hoping would make them wealthy, the abandoned mine stumbled on, no doubt, in the course of one of their trading trips.

Lonzo scratched at a hairless, parchment-like cheek. "We'll believe that when we see the last of you, not before!" Then, dropping his voice to a wheedling note, "And if you've got a drink or two on you, to spare for an old man with the misery in his bones from the rivers we've had to cross — "

Effie interrupted him, "Goddam it, shut up, you old rip! Because we've got things to worry about, even more than what this jasper might do!"

She was pointing down the slope which fell away southward from the mine. Looking that way, Lassiter saw horsemen beginning to flow out of shielding timber. Men and a woman — Amy Follard, sitting saddle in breeches. Besides Amy, Lassiter glimpsed a woman riding beside a familiar, burly figure, and he realized Stag Durkee and Lurie were yonder, also.

It was Mungo's bunch, and Stag had joined them. It was a move Lassiter would never have expected, not from one as experienced and battle-wise as Stag, who knew well the odds against ever collecting anything from such as those.

"Glory!" Lonzo exclaimed, squinting hard toward the riders. "Who be they? And what are they all doing here?"

If not for the arrival of Lonzo and Effie on the scene, Lassiter would likely have been gone by now and since it had been his intent to head directly for the junction of the two rivers, he might well have cut across the front of Mungo's outfit, evading conflict entirely.

He saw Kershaw appear down-slope, look up toward the mine, then call some order. The riders promptly began to spread out in line, facing up-slope.

Effie suddenly cried, "They ain't going to grab what's ours, either!"

She whipped up her rifle and pulled trigger. Range, light and the rather extreme down-angle all mitigated against much hope of accuracy, but Lassiter saw a horse jump, stung by the bullet, and fight its bit.

Lightning streaked again, and thunder cannonaded. A deluge seemed imminent.

Mungo's bush beard appeared. He was conferring with Kershaw, then drawing away, toward a far end of the line of riders. Next, Lassiter saw a flourish of Kershaw's arm. The man gripped a sabre, lifted high.

"My God! He's ordering a charge!" Lassiter exclaimed.

It seemed unbelievable. He almost laughed — a cavalry charge up that slope, some eight or ten riders coming hell for leather, all to overwhelm Lassiter, an addled old man, and a thin, gawky girl.

The line of riders was beginning to

move at the walk. They would rise to the trot, then to the run. Kershaw was out in front, sabre held high. Mungo was off on the right flank. About two minutes from now, Lassiter estimated, they would be here, and a minute after that the odds were high that he would be dead.

10

THERE were moments when Lassiter knew he must act at his best speed — which was considerable — and other moments when he must be deliberate rather than fast, ignoring the cruel pressure of seconds pouring at flood speed toward some shattering event.

This was one of those latter moments. All thoughts, nerves, reflexes operating smoothly but in tight control, he studied that line of advancing riders for perhaps half a breath while considering a number of responses to the cavalry charge.

Finally, ignoring the charge, he turned toward the Moots wagon.

Striding to its rear, he jerked at the cords in a slovenly fastening there and pulled the canvas aside.

As he had hoped, that keg of blasting powder which he had glimpsed by firelight in Plumas, had been loaded last. This was usually the case, to use its weight in balancing the rest of the wagon-load. And it had two companions.

Lassiter lifted the keg out and set it gently on the ground. Then he looked at Lonzo and snapped his fingers. "The fuses? Hand them over, old man — fast!"

"Huh?" Lonzo gabbled. "No, you don't! we need that stuff, for where we're going to sink a shaft — !"

Effie shoved him aside. "Let those lobos keep coming, we'll be wearing white nightgowns and playing harps!" she said. "You're overdue for that, you old coot, but me, I'm planning on living a while yet!"

Reaching into the wagon, she brought out a coil of what looked like fat waxed twine. Lassiter produced his knife and cut off a segment about six inches long.

A glance down slope showed the riders coming on at the trot. Kershaw was still in front, waving his sabre overhead, no doubt regretting that when his blade dipped down there would be no bugler to make thrilling music.

"I guess you know fuses are mighty tricky." Effie said. "That one you're planning to use might take a couple of minutes to burn down or the fire might flash through it so fast you'll blow us all to kingdom come quicker than we can blink."

Lassiter nodded. He punched a hole through thick paper which was glued over the touch-hole at one end of the keg. He would much have preferred to cut off a sample and touch flame to it for a test. As matters stood, he could hope for only about a thirty-second burn from the length he was now inserting in the keg.

Lighting a match and holding it ready, he said, "Grab Lonzo and get away from here!"

She hesitated. Kershaw's sabre dipped down so it thrust straight forward. A menacing roar burst from the riders' throats as they sank spurs deep, lifting their horses to the run. Amy and Lurie had been left behind, Lassiter noticed — and

Stag was not among those in the charge, either.

"Do as I say, girl!" Lassiter shouted. Then he fired the fuse.

It sputtered, burning briskly but not too fast — maybe even less than a thirty-second burn, Lassiter thought hopefully as he lifted the keg. It was heavy, eighty pounds or more. He heaved it up to arm's-length over his head. Guns were beginning to bark in the line of charging horsemen, with a hissing of bullets, but he had to risk being hit in order to delay just a moment longer, and a moment beyond that, while counting seconds in his head.

They were a quarter-mile away, and the range closing fast. But he waited, still counting — until, twenty seconds and more gone since the touch of flame to the fuse, he hurled the keg from him, seeing it hit the ground and roll, bouncing high, then rolling again, spinning down the slope.

A startled medley of yells burst from the oncoming horsemen. They could see

151

it — and the sputtering of the short fuse. The rhythm of the charge began to falter. Kershaw shouted some order to steady them, sabre whirling about his head.

Lassiter fought the urge to crouch with an arm up to shield his eyes. Instead, he turned back to the wagon.

The explosion came as a violent, shuddering wrench of the earth with an eye-searing flash of red fire. An instant later, the shock wave hit like the thrust of a giant hand. Lassiter had to brace himself against it.

A great cloud of black smoke boiled high, mixed with dust swept up by the blast. Through that obscuring pall, he had glimpses of horses bolting this way and that in terror. The charge had been broken, at least for now. Lassiter lifted both of the other kegs of powder out of the wagon and began to cut fuses for them.

He was measuring shorter lengths, figuring twenty-second burning times, when Effie approached him again. "Goddamn, what an explosion!" the girl said. "But you didn't pick none of 'em off, that I could see. I stuck lead in one, though, with my Henry. Gimped him in the leg."

Lassiter had not heard her fire. The sound of her shot had been drowned by the roar.

The smoke and dust were being whisked away by a hard wind. Squinting down-slope, he saw Kershaw and Mungo, both dismounted, conferring. Stag Durkee, also on foot, was moving near them. Stag said something with a gesture toward Lassiter, then a swing of his arm eastward.

Mungo turned his back on Stag in a demeaning and disdainful gesture. The bush-bearded man was speaking to Kershaw, who cupped hands to his mouth, calling an order. The other riders began slowly to form a line once more; some of them were returning from where they had bolted into timber.

Lassiter smiled thinly. "Stag, how do you like it now?" he asked aloud.

"Huh?" Effie said blankly.

Lassiter guessed that Stag had suggested the sensible alternative to another charge — a holding action by some of them to pin Lassiter down and movement by the others to get behind him and strike with the up-slope advantage in their favor.

Mungo had instantly dismissed Stag's suggestion. He had ordered Kershaw to form up the bunch for another charge. This was how Lassiter read it. He quickly but carefully set fuses in the other two powder kegs.

He spoke to Effie, "Cut your mules out of harness; get ready to mount up and ride. We go as soon as I give that bunch another — bigger — taste of hell."

Lonzo, shuffling his feet in the near background, heard this and cried out in agitated alarm, "Give up all that it took us a year of scraping and scratching to put together? Well, we ain't doing it! We're staying right here, even if those mangy dogs come and chew us up — !"

"Which they'll be right obliging about doing — to you, at least," Lassiter interrupted. "They'll likely have different ideas where the girl is concerned."

Effie showed a sudden, decided change of expression. For once, her bravado and feistiness, were muted.

"I'll give you the money to buy a new rig, fresh supplies — a thousand dollars, cash in hand — " Lassiter replied.

It was a prospect that made Lonzo's eyes widen. "By hell, you really mean it? Why that's more cash than I've ever had at one time in the past forty years! I can buy me a whole case of sweet burley eating tobacco — and a barrel of rye whiskey — !"

Then, as Effie glared at him, he added quickly, "Also, a store-bought dress for you, honey, with plenty of frills, lace and ribbons — !"

"Damn it, enough talk!" Lassiter said. "Move! Grab what you can, fast. A blanket apiece, not much more than that. Get those mules ready to ride, and as soon as these kegs blast, head out. Ride straight west. I'll be close behind you."

It was no act of charity on his part to take both of them along in his effort to make it back to Plumas. They would likely be as tiresome as burrs under his hide, but there was a use to be made of Lonzo.

He squinted down-slope again. That line of riders was now re-formed. The men leaning into the hard wind, Kershaw, sabre point high, was haranguing them again in a thin, high-pitched voice. He was like some other Army men Lassiter had known, rebuffed in an ill-advised move but mulishly returning to try the same thing again. Perhaps the decision was Mungo's, but Kershaw was out in front, with Mungo off at a flank again; Stag Durkee was staying well back, refusing to take part in what he no doubt regarded as stupid foolishness.

The line began to come forward, at the walk again, then at the trot. Handguns were working again, winking dots of flame, and the sounds of the shots was overwhelmed by an avalanche of thunder that seemed to cascade down from the sky. Bullets were flying all around and Lassiter was nakedly exposed. Still, he was under iron compulsion to wait, to pick exactly the right fractional instant of time for striking back.

Lonzo and Effie passed behind him, mounted on the mules. Both animals were squealing in protest about having to pack riders. When they headed off westward at a ragged canter, Effie's legs were bare almost to her hips. It would have been a pretty sight at almost any other time.

Lassiter struck a match, cupped the flame in his hands while gauging the rapidly narrowing distance as the attackers whipped their mounts to the run, up the slope.

He bent to fire first one fuse, then to the other. As they sputtered furiously, he picked up a keg, lifted it high, as before, sent it spinning down the slope. Then he grabbed the other also, once more counting the seconds, knowing he was drawing it out very fine. There was no fuse showing outside the third and final leg from the Moots' supplies as he lifted it and heaved it down the slope straight at those making the run at him.

They were beginning to break, again at the sight of the kegs bounding down toward them. Only Kershaw was coming on, sabre extended level before him again. Even Mungo, out at the flank, was veering away, bending down, spurring his mount hard to gain distance.

Lassiter sprinted away too, past the wagon and on toward the motte of alders. Toes digging into loose soil, leaning against the wind, he almost made the cover of those trees when the first explosion came with a fierce buffet of force that almost slammed him flat. The second shattering roar came before the echoes of the first had died away.

In the timber, finding his horses squealing and fighting their ties in fright, he twisted about for a hurried look. At first, there was only another cloud of smoke and dust which covered almost the whole slope. The cloud eddied and boiled, resisting the wild wind, and then in this instant the heavens seemed to open with a deluge pouring down with waterfall force, and the scene rapidly began to clear.

Lassiter released both horses, swung to saddle on the chestnut, and heeled it from cover. As he rode between wagon and mine, bearing west, he had a glimpse of the slope through driving rain.

It was deserted. There was no one in sight down to the timber. The slope was pitted and scarred from the explosions. A dead horse, which Lassiter regretted, was about a quarter of the way down, and also an object which had been Kershaw, and he felt no regret whatever about that. On the whole, it had been a kind of fighting for which he had no liking, and he was glad it was over. The marauders were driven well back for the moment, and the way was open for him to get clear.

Or — was it over? Flame spurted among the trees down-slope; someone was trying a long chance shot at him. Lassiter whipped up his Winchester and sent three fast bullets lashing back.

He had no sense of scoring a hit. Maybe it was an impulsive waste of bullets which he might need later on. Nevertheless, he felt better as he spurred the chestnut to a faster pace. Gun against gun was his idea of the proper way to fight.

The force of that rain slackened, but the rain itself continued. The afternoon was heading toward a wet, dreary night. Lassiter covered a good three miles before he caught up with the clumping mules, still complaining about being ridden.

Effie was wrapped in a sodden blanket with her stringy hair about her face. Lonzo had lost his hat; his bald knob of a head was glisteningly wet.

There had been no sign of pursuit thus far and none was visible as Lassiter looked back. There were only a few more minutes until darkness, when even that Indian, if he was following along, would find tracking them down an impossible task. Lassiter spurred close to Lonzo. "Listen good, now: You're going to get us back to Plumas, but stay away from the Kiskadee, use every short cut and old trail available."

Scratching his inconsiderable chin, Lonzo protested, "You didn't say anything about that when you promised us the thousand dollars for buying new supplies!"

"You want to stay on your own, and let those wolves run you down?" Lassiter began. "Look," he added quickly, "if we're in Plumas by tomorrow night, I'll pay an extra five hundred dollars. A deal — ?"

Effie made some sound at this. Lonzo replied, "Well, I don't know. Plumas is a mighty far piece to be reached in only that amount of time — "

"Shut up!" Effie said. "We'll be there, all right, for that amount of money! And when it's paid . . . I'm going to get me that dress and put up my hair and walk up the street and see to it everybody kow-tows to me!"

Using her Henry rifle, no doubt, to shoot those who didn't, Lassiter thought ironically. And a red dress, probably;

immature females and Indians always were suckers for anything red.

So the journey out of the raw wilderness began through rain and wet. The whole country was becoming a bog. The creeks were overflowing. It was as tiresome a trip as any that had ever been forced on Lassiter.

He kept them going until late and made camp in a lodge-pole thicket, allowing only a small fire which sputtered weakly, giving out not much of either heat or light.

Sometime past midnight, half-dozing, under a dank blanket, he became aware of Effie, suddenly bending to him, a figure of shadowed ivory. She plucked at his blanket, with obvious intent to share it.

Lassiter growled, "Girl, forget it. Go put something on, before you catch your death of cold."

"You saw too much of me, when I was pretty near naked," Effie informed him. "So now I'm your woman."

He snorted at this novel concept.

"Grow up. Three years from now, maybe yes. Right now, no. Hustle back to your bed. Vamoose!"

"Why, Goddam you!" she whispered. "I'm more of a woman than any you ever met, or are ever likely to — !"

She went away, but he had a sense of her, wrapped in her own blanket, somewhere beyond the fire, beyond Lonzo's bubbling snores, and a further sense of her staying awake, baleful regard fixed on him.

Lassiter sighed in exasperation. He was using the packsaddle as a pillow. It seemed these two had heard more gossip than anyone else in this country, so they undoubtedly had heard about the Army and Indian post money, and might make some attempt to take it away from him.

He gave up trying to sleep, putting that off until some time after reaching Plumas. Before first light, he had them up and on the move again, waving both ahead, with a premonition of one of the longest days of his life. And he did not mean for the girl to be in any position where she might impulsively turn her rifle his way.

They slogged along through another day of heavy clouds and constant drizzle. There was no way to figure directions, and the old coot leading, might be heading anywhere.

The day crawled, as Lassiter had anticipated, with few rest stops, a halt at approximately noon for a meagre meal of scraps from his saddlebags, and Effie watching him in sultry anger.

At long last another night came. Still they crawled on. The drizzle continued. Lassiter could not remember having been so soggy before.

Lonzo said, "We're getting close — almost there, by hell! At least . . . I think so."

Then — at midnight or thereabouts lights appeared as blobs before them in the watery dark.

With the rain beginning to come down hard again, in slanting sheets, Lassiter spurred to beside Lonzo. "Swing wide around the town; head for that riverboat," he ordered.

From one side, Effie said, "Listen, we're at the town which is all you asked and we promised. We want our money!"

"You'll get it." He did not intend to have them loose in Plumas with a fat wad of cash before he was gone, to stir up all of the toughnuts at him in an effort to grab the rest of it.

They plodded along some muddy, empty back street toward the roar of the river. Lonzo stopped. Lassiter saw several more lights, reflected in the dark, pock-marked current. He realized those lights were on the *Aurora.*

At sight of them, Lassiter's nerves began to tingle. It was a warning of danger, lurking somewhere. It might be true or might not, but Lassiter always gave serious heed to such a feeling of alarm.

He said, "Wait here, you two."

Dismounting, he brought out his .44, worn under his shirt through the wet, in an effort to keep it reasonably dry. He wanted to be on his feet rather than sitting a saddle if guns suddenly exploded at him.

Taking a step away from the chestnut, then another step, he tried to focus through the rain and blackness on the *Aurora*'s decks. It was then he was hit from behind, violently, without warning. An arm like an oak branch clamped his throat, a knee smashed his back with intent to break it.

11

THE roar of the river and the pounding rain combined to provide complete cover for the attacker, who grunted in harsh triumph as he whipsawed the arm at Lassiter's throat and withdrew his knee for another wicked ramming of his backbone.

Surprise or no, however, Lassiter managed to react very fast. First, he had twisted his body far enough so that the blow from the bony knee missed his spine and spent itself against corded muscle. Now he reached with his free left hand to the arm clamping him from behind, but not to try to break that hold or to claw in an effort to force the other man to relinquish it.

Instead, he gripped the elbow joint, with his fingers like pincers, the nails digging deep. Next, a furious twist applied agonizing pressure to nerves and tendons in what is one of the most sensitive areas of the human body.

The effect was instant and inevitable. Lassiter's antagonist screamed in pain, letting the throttling hold go with a sense of momentary paralysis in the whole lower arm. It was an involuntary move. The arm fell away, and Lassiter spun around at him, with a flick of the .44 at his face — not a full blow, designed to lay him out senseless for an indefinite period. Instead, iron rapped flesh and bone with a sharp clicking sound.

Off-balance and staggering already, the man fell hard. He lay on his belly in mud, limbs jerking, for the moment unable to rise, or to lift his face from a puddle of water. Lassiter toed him over onto his back.

A faint wash of light from a lantern on the *Aurora* showed the scarred, skinned face of the one-time Private, Jay Suggs. Lassiter fought the temptation to stick a bullet in him, then to heave him into the river.

It might be the way, presently, to

rid himself of the man, but until then maybe good use could be made of him. Lassiter reached down, gathered a fistful of wet shirt-front, jerked Suggs up to his feet.

The man's head lolled. A dark, curling worm of blood dribbled from the corner of his mouth. Lips pulled back in a grimace of hate, showing a gap where several teeth had been only moments ago. And his eyes, though unsteady, showed full awareness.

Lassiter shook him. "Who else is staked out, waiting for me to come along? Where?"

Apparently that other bunch had traveled hard and fast, too — and was now also here in Plumas.

Suggs refused to reply. Lassiter shook him again, then reached to touch gun-iron gently against already swelling, torn lips. "You want to swallow the rest of your teeth, just keep on playing dumb with me!"

The man talked now, blood spraying from his mouth, "Twenty-five thousand for my share, including what Benjy would have got, and I'm about to tip you off, maybe help you wind up big winner? Like hell!"

Lassiter said, "Benjy? Your brother, looking a deal like you, who boarded that boat at War Path Landing, then went for a swim in the river — ?"

"That's who!" Suggs said. "It'll take you dead to even things up — a slow, hard dying!"

So the question of one seeming ghost was cleared up. Before Lassiter could prod for more information, including a reply to the question he had asked, Effie Moots was beside him. "Whatever you're meaning to do with this jasper, it can wait. Me and Lonzo want our money, now, so we can find some place out of the wet and start drying off."

She was obviously as soaked through as was Lassiter himself.

Suggs spoke again to Lassiter, "We had a hunch you'd be showing here, along with this gal and the old man — saw them lighting out just before you blew those last two kegs of giant, there by that wore-out mine, tried hard to catch up with you three, but couldn't. It figured, though, that you'd have to come to Plumas, so we just moved faster and got here ahead of you."

Lonzo now chimed in, "Being smart about such things, I figured quick what you had to have in your packsaddle. So me and Effie'll just help ourselves to the cash you promised — "

"Ah, Christ!" Lassiter said.

The words were spoken gently, as a sort of commentary on the way everything was going at this dark and rainy hour — a hot-tempered girl and an old man who showed a weak sort of foxiness at times, nagging at him until he felt scraped raw . . . and a murderous hellion who had turned loquacious all of a sudden to focus Lassiter's attention on himself and away from something else.

What? He had no idea, but he did not intend to spend more time pressuring the information out of Suggs — though he could, in ways to make the pinching of those elbow nerves pleasurable by comparison.

Instead, he would now make use of him, as he had figured a moment ago that perhaps he might.

Reaching to grip Sugg's shirt-front again and to jerk him close, Lassiter struck once more, a swift punching blow aimed precisely just under one ear, crunching the carotid artery, rendering Suggs dazed again.

He sagged and would have fallen if Lassiter had not caught and held him up. Spinning the man around, he stood behind him. Then he spoke, to Effie, "You, girl, come here. Get out of your blanket; wrap it around this hombre. Move!"

His gun was at her, a threat she saw clearly and for once Effie did not have her rifle in hand. Features working stormily in protest, she began to obey.

"And you, Lonzo!" Lassiter continued. "Get the pack-saddle open. Bring out the three satchels you'll find in it. Carry them aboard the boat, forward."

He took off his hat, clapped it on Suggs' head, the brim pulled down. "Now," he continued to Effie, "We're going to walk this one aboard, too. Take hold. Let him lean on you."

She said, "If I only had my Henry, so I could tell you where to go — and get you started — !"

They shuffled toward the *Aurora*, Suggs with his head down, feet dragging, Lassiter hoping that anyone else of that bunch glimpsing them might think Suggs was himself, Lassiter, and that he was Suggs though he was not about to bet this proposition too strongly.

However, it didn't seem there could be so very many of them, maybe eight or nine, including both Mungo and Stag Durkee, and with the whole town to cover they might be spread out rather thinly, perhaps not too much reason to fear attack from another of them here beside the river.

Maybe this reasoning was right; they stepped from wharf to boat deck, just forward of the cabin structure, hauling

Suggs with them, no sign of danger developing. It was quite dark. He released his hold, Effie did the same, and Suggs folded down to splintery deck planking.

The tingling of nerves, again, told Lassiter there could be more danger on the boat than there had been on the wharf. He looked up to lights showing in the wheelhouse, then aft to another bright glow about half-way back, the boat's cargo area.

He said, "Lonzo, get started in that direction. I'll be right behind you, so don't try anything at all that might make me think you're figuring a cute scheme to collect more than I owe you. Move slow. Hang onto those satchels."

Bending, Lassiter hauled Suggs to his feet again, this time with a grip at the scruff of his neck. "You're not that much out, so walk. Stay close to the old man's heels."

Suggs began to shamble as ordered, Lassiter retaining his grip on the man, gun alert, touching Suggs' cheek with it at each step as a reminder.

He had taken only two of those steps when he suddenly realized he had erred. Seriously? This remained to be seen; and the error was that he had let Effie take herself away. She had vanished as quietly as a shadow.

Increasing the pace, Lassiter shoved Suggs brusquely along she river side of the deck between cabin structure and rail.

He was banking that if he encountered anyone, it would be in the lighted cargo area, that any of the bunch who might be aboard would have no reason to be up at the wheelhouse or on this side of the boat.

Like all theories, though, it might not be true. The feel of danger was growing stronger in Lassiter with each step — and unsteady steps they were, since the boat was constantly in motion, dipping, rising under his feet, battered constantly by the river.

There was light ahead in cargo area, open all the way across the boat. Lonzo Moots had almost reached it, hugging the three satchels with Suggs close on his heels as ordered, when a man stepped out onto the deck, someone bulky in silhouette, peering toward the three and exclaiming, "Hey, Suggs, you caught up with them — and the cash? Hot damn!"

Then, still speaking, he saw Lassiter coming into the fan of light; he spat a frantic obscenity and tried to draw a gun belted at his hip.

Lassiter fired with cold intent. He meant to cut the force against him by at least one man. But the boat lurched, and he hit the man's arm and the fellow was flung back inside, his gun flying over the boat rail, into the river.

Hurling Suggs headlong before him, then grabbing Lonzo Moots and dragging him fully into that cargo area before shoving him aside also, Lassiter confronted them all by lantern-light.

Four of them — Cap'n Strunk first, mopping his jowls; then Lurie, toward the wharf side of this wide, empty cargo space here; Amy Follard, sitting on a wooden box, head down but snapping up as she stared at Lassiter; and finally, the man with the bushy beard, holding a long-barreled Cavalry Colt, pointed at Strunk — now starting to swing it toward Lassiter, who said, voice as hard and as cold as deep winter ice, "Hold it! You quit or die, this moment. Decide quick which it is to be . . . Colonel Follard!"

It had come to this, in a sudden intuitive flash, that everything he knew, added together — beginning with the other Suggs calling this man 'sir' on that other night above-decks, and Amy being with him in her nightgown — must result in only one answer. Also, Lassiter thought, it was to gain time for him that Suggs had turned gabby, out on the wharf. And Lassiter continued, "Drop the gun. I could mash your hand, at this distance, but I won't; instead, I'll blow a hole through your head."

The man glared from eyes which held a wetness of hot bile, but before Lassiter's chill gaze seemed to freeze a little. He let his hand open. His Colt clattered to the floor.

The one who had taken Lassiter's bullet moaned on the floor. Lassiter said, "Your bunch is getting thinned down; cancel out another one — along with Odem, and Kershaw — "

That beard quivered in fury. Colonel Jason Follard said, "A fine, brave young officer, Captain Kershaw, dead by a cheap-jack trick, a hoodlum device, those kegs of powder — !"

"I should have stood still, maybe, to be skewered by his sabre? And I saved him a possible long stay in some Federal prison, charged with desertion — the same charge that's facing you — twenty years, about, at hard labor — "

Everything added up to this. It explained why it had been necessary for Jason Follard to seem to be dead, with someone handy whose identity he could assume, if needed. A hapless Indian trader named Clyde Mungo had filled that part.

"By the Great Jehovah, no!" Follard

cried. "I have endured too much to be balked now — the year of waiting and now all of it almost in my hands — !"

He looked to the three leather satchels, dropped on the floor by Lonzo Moots, and his fingers writhed avariciously.

Lassiter said, "Don't call on the Almighty to back up your thieving and your lies!"

"The world could have been ours; it can still be mine!" Follard said. "It will be Mexico, maybe, or Brazil, or Argentina . . . a General's stars, and the station, the deference denied me in the rag-taggle mob called an Army in this country — !"

"With that gang following along that has been backing your play, each of them hoping for big cuts of the money?" Lassiter inquired. "I doubt it. You would have needed the whole bundle to buy those General's stars with the whole bunch, including Kershaw, short-changed, left empty-handed."

Crouching on the deck planking, Suggs licked his lips. "God, Colonel, tell him he's lying — and tell me I still draw shares for both me and Benjy!"

Mopping his jowls, Cap'n Eli Strunk said "I would've swore my oath he was Clyde Mungo — with that beard. Even up close, when he come shoving that gun at me, saying he was waiting right here, for somebody. You?" And then, "Uh what happens next?"

Still with his penetrating gaze fixed on Follard, Lassiter said, "Strunk, you ready for a trip down-river?"

"Yeah. Was held up by some work on a safety valve. I figured to head back south at first light tomorrow."

"No. Tonight. Right now," Lassiter said.

Strunk's eyes bulged. "That's loco talk! Nobody runs the river at night!"

"You will. There's some eight or ten miles of fairly smooth water just south of here, I remember, no rapids. You'll run your boat that far, at least."

"I'll have to get up steam — !"

"Do that while we're moving."

"I — I — !" Hands flapping in protest.

"I'll make it worth your while. Put a price on the boat. Make it a fair one — fair profit to you and I'll buy, on the spot. Well — ?"

Startled, shaken, abruptly avaricious also, Strunk plucked at a pendulous under-lip. "Uh — five thousand — ?"

"Sold. Cash in hand," Lassiter said. "Lonzo, open that satchel by your left foot. The money inside is in blocks of a thousand dollars each. Hand him five of them."

Lonzo squatted to obey. Follard made a gasping, whining sound. He took a step toward the green paper in its tight blocks. Lassiter rapped gun-barrel sharply against a cheek-bone. He halted, breathing hard.

Holding his money, Strunk said, "So you've bought my boat. But you didn't buy me. I still ain't running the river at night."

"You'll do it — for pay," Lassiter said. "Five hundred more to steer this ramshackle tub down to LeGrande — ?"

Strunk trembled also — tempted, torn

by temptation, with the combined roar of rain and the river abruptly very loud.

"A thousand," Lassiter said. "Hand him that much more, Lonzo."

Strunk gulped hard, accepting another chunk of cash.

Follard said, voice harsh, choked, "You . . . with the red nose and the fat gut . . . you signed your death warrant, taking that money. My money! I guarantee you'll never see daylight again — !"

With a fanatic sheen on his features, the bushy beard jutting, he hurried on, "I shall prevail — against all odds. Against the bitch-whore who sought to destroy me — !" He sent a scorching glance at his wife, still sitting on the box. "And against you, also. I shall see you all dead!"

"Brash talk, Colonel," Lassiter said, "Just what do you aim to do?"

Follard breathed stertorously. "You will see; an instant before destruction strikes you down."

"That sounds as though you must be expecting your bunch ashore to hit this boat, any minute," Lassiter said.

He glanced to Lurie. "Girl, where is Stag?"

Red hair glinting like new copper wire, she replied, "He went to try to buy some stuff — laudanum? — that might help his headache, while he was waiting for you to show."

"Then he's due here, and more to worry about than all the rest of them put together," Lassiter said. "So I'd better get ready, with Follard out of the way somewhere — "

He stopped speaking. Somebody had come in from the deck, the wharf side of the boat, moving at a tempestuous pace. It was Effie Moots, Henry rifle gripped with both hands, shouting, "We get the money right now that you owe me and Lonzo, no more of your fancy talk and putting us off, or for sure you'll be dead and buried — in the river — "

Then she screamed in indignation, for Lassiter had turned toward her. He had no immediate idea how to handle this termagant female, and Follard had snatched at the desperate chance to leap and seize her. Putting Effie in front of him, now, an arm tight about the girl, he started dragging her with him — toward the open door through which she had come.

Lassiter had only a second or so to decide whether he should shoot her in order to get Follard, and he was greatly tempted to do just that.

12

SECONDS flashed past while Lassiter wrestled with his problem: whether to shoot Effie Moots as the only way to get a shot at Colonel Jason Follard.

Given more stable footing and better light, it would not have been a problem, since Follard towered a good head above the girl. Lassiter would have found putting a bullet through that head, as he had already promised to do if the man made trouble no great difficulty. As it was, though, he felt a miss with Effie hit instead, was rather likely.

As to whether she deserved to be shot, this would make for an interesting debate. But then, Lassiter decided against it. She had been a pain and undoubtedly would continue to be so, but no female could be held very accountable for her behavior — and also, she was rather pretty, might develop into something quite desirable. So, his decision was to spare her, and hence, as well, Colonel Jason Follard.

Who, eyes ablaze with exultation above his thicket of a beard, made it to the outer door of the cargo area, dragging Effie with him as a shield. There, he leaped backward into the open, with a harsh shove which sent the girl at a headlong stagger back toward Lassiter. She spun around and sat down hard with an angry, pained yelp.

Meanwhile, there had been hurried, furtive movement. Suggs was going for the opposite door, scrambling on hands and knees. The man Lassiter had shot in the arm was struggling to make it through that door and out, the arm hanging stiffly at his side.

Lassiter let them go. Both Lonzo Moots and Cap'n Strunk were in the way this time and might stop bullets meant for them. They made it out, into darkness and rain.

For an instant there was deep quiet here. Lonzo was standing, holding a block of cash in each hand from the valise he had opened. He teetered, as though about to run. Effie was still sitting, rubbing herself. The other two women were in frozen attitudes. Cap'n Strunk stood, holding the money he had accepted and looking as though wishing he had not so readily agreed to take it.

Lassiter spoke first to Lonzo, "Stick that cash back where you got it."

"You owe us!" the old man squeaked. "I'm only taking what's rightly ours!"

"And some more besides. Stick it back," Lassiter ordered.

Effie cried, "You've put me and Lonzo off long enough!"

Still clutching her rifle, she made a try to swing it at him. Lassiter went at her in two fast strides; he bent to take the Henry from her.

Again, she tried to claw his face. Lassiter slapped her. It was a move which, in his opinion, had been delayed somewhat too long.

Stepping back, he was greatly tempted to throw her gun over the side into the river, as he had threatened at their first meeting. However, with his own Winchester left on the chestnut gelding, at the dock, and with the possibility of a need for every available weapon, he decided against it.

There was some hoarse yelling on shore — Follard summoning his men to attack? In a swift estimate, Lassiter figured he had three to five minutes, no more, before it came. A sharp gesture of his .44 made Lonzo kneel creakily to return the money. At another gesture, Lonzo closed the satchel.

Lassiter glanced to Cap'n Strunk. "You took my money to handle this boat — my boat now," he informed the red-nosed man. "So get up to your wheelhouse and start doing it."

"Well — uh — " Strunk said uncertainly. "I'm not sure how many of the crew are aboard to feed the fire-box — "

"If the answer comes up none, we ride the river with a cold boiler," Lassiter said. "And don't cross me by trying to leave in a pier-head jump, Mister, or you'll find yourself swimming down to LeGrande. Move! About two minutes from now the lines are going to be cast off, the boat will begin to move, and you'd better have that wheel in your hands when it happens."

Strunk took himself off, at a wobbly pace, heading toward a rickety inner stairway leading upward. Lassiter devoted several seconds more to a swift study of those here or, actually, a weighing of Amy Follard and Lurie, with another decision reached, and the pointing of a finger at Amy. "You've got a stake in the cash. Can I trust you to guard it?"

Her eyes seemed questioning, maybe with memory of how she had left the boat at War Path Landing, going to Follard, and also how she had fled from Lassiter, that night after he had freed her. But she moistened her lips and replied, "Yes."

It was not a good arrangement; there was no guarantee he could trust her any more than he could Lurie, but it was the best solution he could seem to come by

189

in the hurry of the moment. He scooped up Follard's long-barreled pistol from the floor and handed it to her.

This done, he started out, the way Follard had gone.

Effie Moots came at him again, arms windmilling. "We aren't going to stay on this damned boat! You're going to pay Lonzo and me, and we're leaving!"

Exasperated to the utmost, he longed to slug her, knock her out — or to up-end Effie, bare her boyish bottom, whack it until it bloomed like Cap'n Strunk's nose. But time was pressing him hard. Lassiter contented himself with cupping a hand under Effie's chin and lifting her up on her toes.

He said, "Follard wouldn't let you off the wharf with as much as a dime of what he regards as all his. You'll be paid at LeGrande . . . if we make it there — "

He let her go, went on out, then, sliding quickly down to one knee, back against a siding, widening eyes quickly for night vision.

The rain seemed to be slackening.

190

The boat shuddered and creaked, shaken roughly by the river. Lassiter was aware of movement along the wharf, quick dartings here and there of shadowy figures, hurried growls of talk.

Someone else came out of the cargo area, to crouch beside him, with a wisp of perfume that he remembered. It was Lurie, breath warm against his cheek as she whispered, "Do you see Stag — or hear him?"

"No. Get back inside, girl, where you'll be safer when bullets fly."

"Not much safer. That side wall won't be a lot better than cardboard at stopping lead."

Above them, on the texas, Lassiter heard Strunk call some order. An answer came from forward in a deep bass voice. Then there was movement, also forward, with sudden spurts of gun-flame on the wharf, bullets fast-triggered, and a yell of fright and dismay from whoever had answered Strunk.

"They've pinned him down," Lurie said. "That strawberry-nosed skipper told him to cast off the for'ard line, but now he's afraid to move."

She stood. "I practically grew up with river boats, back on the big Mizzou. I'll do it."

She ran forward at a light, quick pace.

There was another yell ashore. More bullets began to fly, the winks of flame now like anvil sparks. Lassiter holstered the .44; he swung Effie's rifle and opened up with it, firing at those flashes.

He called, "Stag! That's your girl they're shooting at!"

Maybe Stag shouted something in reply; it was hard to tell. Lassiter felt a sudden sideward lurch as the *Aurora*'s bow was freed of the wharf and shoved out into the river by the Kiskadee's savage current.

It left an aft line still binding the boat to the wharf, however, in spite of what Lassiter regarded as Lurie's astonishing feat of releasing that forward tether. He moved to his left, exposed for a moment by light from the cargo area, with shouts and those guns aiming at him. Maybe four of them altogether, for a quick guess, which indicated Follard didn't have his full bunch here yet.

Hard on this thought, Follard cried, "Get aboard! He's alone — and he has the money; kill him!"

Concerted movement began, all along the wharf, movement toward the boat, as Lassiter left it, leaping from the narrow deck, near the paddles. He bent, feeling hurriedly — found a length of taut rope, as thick as a man's arm, and worked his way to where it was looped around a bollard.

Putting his strength against this rope, he struggled to free it, with a heave, then another heave. The line seemed to move a little. He swore, tonelessly, with a feel of time running out, of being balked, possibly defeated, by this rope.

Then someone came running toward him, with a breathless whisper. "It's me, again!" Lurie thrust something at him. His hand closed on an axe-handle.

"Stand clear!" He swung it, one-handed, undercutting the rope where it rubbed against the bollard. Before him, a strip of widening dark water showed the boat swinging away from the wharf — but as he noted this, a shadow leaped that gap, and another; two of Follard's outfit were on the *Aurora*.

The rain was definitely quitting, now. He heard someone else yell, then run at a pounding pace along the wharf. Another shadow, maybe two more, leaped the space between wharf and boat. Lassiter swung the axe a second time, with care. The rope parted, whipping off into darkness.

He grabbed at Lurie. "Get aboard!"

She was a wriggling armful as he threw her at the deck. He leaped also, barely making it, so quickly had the boat left the wharf.

It was partly to spare her from Follard's wrath, if the man should get his hands on her, partly intent to neutralize Stag, or make him hesitate, should Stag be aboard. Though Lassiter wondered about this, and whether Stag might be vengeful of the two defections. He hauled Lurie to her feet, growling, "Girl, looks like you're mixed up again, whose side you're on!"

"No. All I want is to keep Stag out of trouble. Let me go to him — !"

She struggled to leap back toward the wharf. Lassiter drove her flat. There was no time to explain, or to be gentle; somebody was coming at them, running along this lower stretch of deck, a gun beginning to spit fire, bullets slashing, ricocheting, screaming about Lassiter's face.

Somebody hurrying his shots, hoping for a fast hit that would be more luck than skill, and hence not Stag, who would never be guilty of such stupidity. Lassiter leveled the Henry, held steady, compensated for the way the rifle threw to the right, and he squeezed the trigger.

It was a hit, maybe chest-high, the force of the bullet driving the fellow sideways across the deck and over the railing into the river.

He splashed, vanishing. Another one was behind him, bellying down for a moment, triggering a couple of wild shots, then was up and drawing back. Lassiter heard a brief spate of hurried talk, a pair of them conferring. He spoke to Lurie, "Get back inside!" Then he started forward, suspecting the setting up of a try to come at him from two different directions at once. Those two before him seemed to melt into shadows. A sputtering wheeze came from the *Aurora*'s whistle, indicating some steam in the boiler. The paddles began to turn. Follard shouted from somewhere on the wharf. He sounded half-strangled with rage.

Lassiter went back into the cargo area, where lanterns hung on hooks swayed and danced about with the motion of the boat, casting weird shadows.

Amy was crouching beside the three satchels of cash, gripping the long-barreled pistol. Effie and Lonzo were both flattened down, against the far wall. Five or six guns were roaring ashore, with bullets slashing through the wall on that side of the boat like blind hornets.

Lurie followed Lassiter in. He exchanged a glance with Amy, noting that even the baggy pants she wore could not detract from her feminine appeal. He went fast across the width of the boat and out that opening on the other side, flattened down also in a lizard-like wriggling.

This was to surprise whoever might be working aft toward him on this side of the boat — himself down flat, since most men were slaves to the habit of looking for a man to appear through a door or around a corner at eye level.

The Henry was forward, ready for instant use. But he had no target; the deck forward on this side showed empty.

It suggested a possibility which he was sure must be right, a try to get at him by way of the overhead deck where the staterooms were located.

It was easy enough to go up the stairway forward, to that deck, aft along it, down to this deck aft, in a move to hit him from behind. And Lassiter was up and moving instantly himself with this thought, running aft, on his toes, with a minimum of sound — past the boat's boiler-room, where somebody laboring at the fire-box, feeding chunks of wood, gawked at him for a moment, eyes and teeth very white in a dark face.

The framework for the *Aurora*'s big paddle-wheel loomed above him, the paddles now slapping the water harder, faster. That framework was as high as the boat's full three decks. Lassiter shoved the Henry barrel down one pants-leg, leaped to grab a cross-beam with both hands, and swung himself up, climbing fast.

It was something that had to be done with care — lose his grip, fall in among those paddles and he would be battered swiftly into bloody mush. And if he was spotted in this climb, he might be picked off at leisure, even by someone who was less than a crack shot.

But he made it to the cabin deck, swung himself over the railing there, put his feet on solid flooring — and someone swore in gleeful surprise, then rushed him from forward, yelling, "I've got the bastard, Colonel — !"

This assailant pulled trigger as he came, flame scorching Lassiter's face. Narrowly, he missed. Lassiter was still alive. The Henry came out of his pants-leg as he put his feet on the deck; he dodged, leaped to close quarters, the rifle's stock forward, all of his sinewy strength behind its ramming force.

A shock ran up his arm, with a feel of bone crunching and splintering under that smash of hardwood. The other man mouthed some sound of agony, and Lassiter had an impression of a face that had instantly become a mask of blood. The man was falling forward, his hand pawing, dragging a gun barrel against Lassiter's temple.

The blow rocked him. He staggered aside as the man crashed down before him; he slammed hard against a cabin wall and recoiled from that against the railing, almost going over it into the water. The deck seemed to drop under his feet. For a moment, all coordination lost and knowing this, Lassiter tried with his most determined effort of will to recover his wits, and could not do so.

Then somebody came around a corner from the rear of the boat — the same corner around which Suggs had leaped at him that other night at War Path Landing. This man tonight paused, swore in harsh exultation, lunged on at Lassiter.

A voice from behind Lassiter said, "*Amigo*, looks like you ran yourself into a corner at last that you can't get out of — !"

Lassiter turned his head with grinding effort. From one side, that man was coming at him. On the other side, a little way forward, he saw Stag Durkee, gun bearing directly at Lassiter with a tight grin above the gun and a flaring of Stag's eyes, which said he was pulling trigger.

13

LASSITER had known many moments — almost too many to recall — when he had been a half-breath or less from death. This was such a moment, perhaps the most dangerous ever. A killer was at his back, Stag Durkee before him, with the blaze of Stag's eyes warning of a bullet to come. To think of him missing at such a distance was impossible.

All of this as Lassiter staggered, still in the grip of vertigo resulting from the drag of the gun barrel against his temple — and his grim reflection was that he was finished. His only hope was to cling to life for a second, a pair of seconds, long enough to insure that he put a bullet into Stag, finishing him also.

Though . . . mighty damned scant satisfaction in accomplishing such a feat, and with a very puzzling question which might never be answered: Why in the hell would Stag come at him in such a manner, knowing the high likelihood of dying himself, only for the satisfaction of dealing Lassiter out?

There was an answer, however, and it came before even one of the seconds had passed, as Stag shifted his gun, a shift so faint as to be almost imperceptible, and fired past Lassiter, with the plunge of his bullet into the man who was coming at him from behind.

The chunk of that bullet driving deep into flesh, the wheeze of breath rushing from shattered lungs, the crash as the man spilled down to the deck all of these sounded very loud to Lassiter, who now saw Stag turn aside and lean against the rail, scrubbing his face roughly with the heel of his hand, gun sagging down. And Lassiter, shaking his own head, feeling it begin to clear, the wave of vertigo passing, tried to figure out now why it had worked out this way.

He said, essentially the same question

asked of Lurie, "Stag, who in the hell are you siding, anyway?"

"Well, not the pack of mongrels I got mixed up with in the sorriest move of my life," Stag muttered in reply. "Lurie warned me in advance it would be a mistake. There is a girl who sees things a damned sight clearer than I've been doing lately. Matter of fact, I haven't been seeing anything very good."

He shook his head, apparently also to clear it. "I'll probably have to start wearing glasses," Stag continued. "Can't you just see me, a pair of specs perched on my nose? By God, it'll likely be the end of Stag Durkee! — especially with my luck so bad anyway, lately, no deal I've tried for months coming close to working out — "

There was a morose, dreary sound in his voice. But he added, "The hell with all that, though. As for who I'm siding with, it's been burning in me I had to make a change, get away from that fellow with his face hid by all those whiskers — high odds he meant to deal me out with a bullet in the back, soon as he closed his fist on what he wanted. So I switched from backing his play to backing you."

"So, thanks," Lassiter responded. "You won't get a bullet in the back from me, Stag — but you won't get anything else from me, either, aside from a ride on this boat to wherever it's going."

Vivid in memory was the night beside that fire and Stag's cold, hard proposal to finish him off. He would grant the man something for saving his life moments ago, since it seemed that had happened, but he was not about to trust him. Not for a while yet, at least.

"*Seguro,*" Stag said. "I'd handle it exactly the same way if I was standing in your boots. And we're not home free, by any means; it might still be the dying with no burying for both of us — "

As if to emphasize what he was saying, the firing ashore, which had started to die away behind them, suddenly stepped up in volume, accompanied by ferocious yells, several men running along the bank and pulling trigger fast, with bullets hissing, chunking the boat hard.

And before Lassiter could offer any comment, the man who had taken the rifle butt with blood spurting from his face now abruptly surged up again, with some hoarsely gobbled obscenity, to make a fast try again to kill Lassiter.

But Lassiter, steadiness in him anew, poured two bullets at him before he could fire — and this time, as he crumpled down, there was no doubt he was dead.

"Christ! If he had been trying for me," Stag muttered, "it would have been my finish all right and no damned mistake whatever, since all I could see of him was a blur. And we'd better be sure the other one don't get up to try making any more trouble, either."

He bent and used his gun, a further roar in the night, and several more guns were now crashing along the river bank.

Lassiter growled, "Help me get rid of them. Then we're putting the boat between us and Follard's guns. Meanwhile, Stag, any more of his bunch on board — ?"

"Not that I know of," Stag grunted, as they lifted first one body and then the other, sliding them over the railing into the river. "It's hard to tell, though, since I'm not sure just how many are backing him — heard talk about several in Plumas ready to join up if there was a real good chance at that cash; also, recruiting any number of toughnuts with nothing else to do wouldn't be much of a trick."

Leaning against the rail, Stag continued, "I'd say his original bunch has been pretty well used up, but you sure aren't rid of him. He kited ashore himself, to give orders and send whoever was handy running at the boat to finish you off. Don't make the mistake of thinking he's a coward, though. Instead, he's hipped on thinking in the military way, which says a high-ranking officer stays back and tells the troops to do the dirty work. If it comes down to you and him at the end, though, he won't back off."

"Head forward, Stag," Lassiter said. "In front of me."

"Okay. Be careful of your footing," Stag muttered, "because of the blood. It's something I never seemed to notice before; God, there's a lot of blood in a man!"

"Stay in front of me," Lassiter said. "I won't like it a damned bit if you're ever behind me."

A long way to LeGrande, he thought, and a clever, devious, unscrupulous man tramping before him; maybe he'd make it with no more trouble from Stag Durkee, but logic said it wouldn't be smart to bet that way.

The boat was thrashing fairly steadily along now, though shivering in every beam. Ashore, the red streakings of gunfire were diminishing, falling away behind them in the black night. With Follard just maybe shaken off for good, but Lassiter wouldn't risk a red cent betting on that, either. He felt a strong hunch that his path and Follard's would cross again — violently.

Somewhat more than an hour later, he was again in the stateroom he had occupied heading north. Lassiter had shaved, then stripped down and washed himself. Now, a towel wrapped about his middle, he lighted a dusty stogy from a box turned up in the boat's pantry.

He had a full stomach. It had developed that Lurie was rather a good cook. After fussing over Stag and scolding him, she had turned to fixing a supper of fried beef and potatoes, beans and tomatoes from cans, cornbread, and coffee for all on board.

Lassiter had prowled the *Aurora* until he was satisfied no ambusher was waiting in a dark corner or a chance at him. He had checked the wheelhouse where Cap'n Strunk was sweating copiously. "Maybe I can find Ten Mile Cove in the dark and tie up there until daylight," Strunk had opined hopefully.

"How far south is that?" Lassiter had demanded.

"Like the name says, ten miles."

"Too close to Plumas. Keep going."

"I can't risk the rough water that begins just beyond, without being able to see fifty yards, any direction!"

"You can't spend that cash of yours in hell, either — or in purgatory, and you'll land in one of them if you tie up where that bunch after me can take another bite. Keep going!"

Gently drawing on the stogy, Lassiter considered his situation and found it neither good nor bad. He was alive, functioning, and he demanded no more from fate. As for tomorrow . . . But Lassiter, a complete fatalist, seldom wasted any time speculating about the future.

He had what had drawn him into this country, the three satchels of money, stowed in the stateroom's upper bunk. He meant to retain his possession of them, until the moment when he could turn two of the satchels over to Anson Brett.

And, after that . . . Lassiter hummed gently, refusing to anticipate what might occur then, turning his thoughts instead to an event in the immediate future that he could anticipate with both certainty and pleasure — thinking of Amy Follard.

He wondered if the woman was also in the same stateroom she had used on the trip north. But while he was wondering, a knock sounded at his door.

Likely the pesty chit, Effie Moots, he decided; she had been at him like a gadfly ever since he had walked into the cargo hold again, keeping Stag Durkee carefully ahead of him. She wanted the money due her and Lonzo, wanted her rifle back, wanted for them to be put ashore so they could walk to Plumas, and the hell with riding the boat to LeGrande.

Now, Lassiter suspected, in her mercurial fashion she could be wanting again to slide under some blankets with him. As he growled, "Come in!" it was with an exasperated determination to upend her at last, spank the girl's firm bottom until it flamed rosy red.

The door opened. It was Amy, slipping quickly in, wrapped rather awkwardly in a coarse and not very clean sheet, sitting down at the lower bunk, trying to arrange the sheet's folds — than, as with a shrug, as though to indicate it could not matter very much, letting it slip away from her.

Staring at him, at the shadows of several old scars on his chest, she said, "I — I felt we had to talk, but I don't know where to begin."

One thing was certain, he thought somewhat sardonically, she represented no danger to him, since she certainly did not have Follard's long-barreled pistol on her. "Talk? Sure. Speak out, whatever is on your mind."

"Well — your telling me I could still have a share of the money, after my idiocy of running away from you, twice over, the night when we first met here and that other night when the man Durkee showed up with his . . . girl. And if you were to ask me why I behaved like that — "

She spread her hands a little. "All I can say is that when I see his eyes, when he speaks, I feel — mesmerized. Even when I know he is near, I can't resist. So I went to him, both times."

She brooded over this. "Even though he threatens to kill me, and I thought he might do it, in his rage, that night when he was tearing off my nightgown. Also, he threatens to turn me over to other men, to be brutalized by them, since he has suspected me, accused me of cheating on him, since our wedding."

It was a picture of a marriage poisoned by suspicion and hate. She said, "I'll never be free until he is dead — or I am. If you hadn't found the money, I think he would have forced its location from me. And then handed me over to his men or killed me? I don't know . . . "

She brooded over this. The lamplight showed warm tones of cream and ivory in her opulent figure. "He had dreams of glory, but was born too late for the war with the south, when other men won their stars. His permanent rank was only Lieutenant Colonel, and he began to realize he would not go any higher, would never be a General in the Army. That was when he decided to steal the money. And I realized there could be no place for me in his life if he got away with it; he would discard me, at the least — or kill me. I had to act for myself!"

Lassiter smoked reflectively, checking the boat's continuing movement southward. "How did you come by the money?"

"It was taken from the ambulance the morning of the crossing of the Brule, carried to the abandoned mine, hidden in the house there — by Suggs."

"Did you know Suggs had a brother, a twin — ?"

"Not then. The brother wasn't in the Army. The Suggs that Jason entrusted with the money — but with the Indian, Lame Wolf, watching him — was the one you threw off this boat at War Path Landing. I managed to leave the ambulance and followed them. I took the money from the house, put it in the tunnel where you found it."

"How did you know about the tunnel?"

"An uncle of mine dug it and the main shaft of that mine, managing to lose all of the family fortune in those holes in the ground, before he died in a cave-in. When I was a little girl, he took me into the tunnel and showed me the door, proud it was so hard to find."

"True enough. Follard didn't find it."

"He didn't even go into the tunnel — sent the Indian to check, instead, and accepted his report of nothing there. Then Jason suddenly began to realize, lately, that that was a mistake. He would probably have found it fairly soon if you hadn't done so, whether he forced me to talk or not."

Lassiter had a final draw on the stogy, discarded it.

Amy said, "He knew I must have grabbed the money, even though he took that house apart, trying to find it, then had to burn the place to cover his search. He had me followed for a while, as I left the country, knew I didn't have the money with me, that it must still be there, somewhere. I was afraid to try running with it then — a mistake; I should have taken it along, no matter the risk."

"But," Lassiter said, "you did take some of it."

"Well, yes, about a thousand dollars. Jason took some also, before sending it to be hidden in the house; he had to have the money, so the enlisted men of his patrol who had thrown in with him could buy their discharges."

This accounted for the bills that had shown up.

Amy said, "The reason the money was moved there and hidden was that Jason had already decided a period of time must elapse before it was divided up. He spoke of six months, then of a year, telling his men to find jobs around Plumas and be patient; he holed up in a cabin north of town. Actually, as they learned the past few days, he was waiting for me to come back — to lead them to the money."

She sighed, wearily. "That almost happened. A telegraph line was recently strung into Plumas, and it brought him word I was on my way to War Path Landing — where he grabbed me."

Lassiter thought of her words. A lunatic sort of deal, he reflected, which was usually the case when amateurs tried to bring off a big steal. Though, in his experience, professionals could botch such a job, also.

Follard might have brought it off, a year ago, save for the meddling of a wife who hated him — ? Lassiter thought, *quien sabe*? He did not like to deal in ifs and maybes. That the dice had not yet come seven for Jason Follard was no guarantee they wouldn't, in the near future. Amy whispered, "Poor Milo Kershaw! He had resigned his commission, dazzled by Jason's talk of glory to be won in some other country — and went to his death in that charge, which Jason ordered but told Milo to lead."

Then, looking up to Lassiter with an impact of tear-damp lustrous eyes, "I don't want to die, like Kershaw. Help me to get free, with the share you promised — !"

It now seemed clear why she had come to him tonight; it was an overt offering of herself for his pleasure, in return for protection; and a moistening of her lips, a sudden feverish quivering of her body, indicated she found the prospect of that far from distasteful.

Lassiter nodded, pleased no further preliminaries would be necessary. He lifted the .44, reached to flip the towel from about his middle.

As he did so, the boat suddenly lurched, with a violence which slammed him against a wall, hurling Amy Follard sideways and almost off the lower bunk. An instant later a medley of startled, frightened yells echoed throughout the boat.

"Go get dressed!" he snapped. "Hurry!"

He was snatching at his own gear,

starting to haul it on, as Amy Follard clutched the sheet to herself and darted through the door.

The boat was at a standstill, grinding sounds rippling through it. It had struck something and might already be tearing itself to pieces.

Finishing by stamping feet into his boots, putting on his hat, he lunged out of the stateroom, only moments behind Amy Follard. With him he took two of the satchels of cash, all he could conveniently handle.

If the *Aurora* was sinking, then of course the game was lost, though; Lassiter doubted if he could get far trying to swim with the two heavy satchels. Not that trying to swim the wild Kiskadee held much hope under any circumstances. He ran forward, down to the main deck, with a sense fate might finally have dealt the black ace of death to all on board.

14

THE lower deck, the *Aurora*'s cargo deck, seemed to tilt outward and down, but the water from the nearby rushing river was not spilling across it, so perhaps there was hope the boat was not in imminent danger of sinking.

Lassiter refused to accept this as more than a chance, however. Swearing at himself for not taking into account the possibility of a grounding — a matter of some unfamiliarity with the dangers of river boats — he looked about, noticed a tarpaulin that had been wadded and shoved under the stairway forward on this, the boat's port side. He pulled the tarp out, shoved the two satchels under the stairs, spread the tarp over them.

There were undoubtedly a hundred better hiding places aboard but Lassiter had no time to check them out. He could only hope this place would serve in case he wanted his hands on those containers of cash again in a hurry.

The task done, he hurried on forward, to check on the yelling. What he discovered was two crewmen, apparently the only ones on board, leaning into two long poles with their muscles bulging, shoving hard at something below the water at the *Aurora*'s bow.

Half-naked, their black skins glistened in the light of a lantern held by Cap'n Strunk, who was peering at the Kiskadee's dark racing flood and snapping orders — confusing, contradictory orders, made more so by the fact he was somewhat drunk. "We're stuck on — h'm — a sandbar," he informed Lassiter. "But don't worry; we'll soon sh'shove her free."

Effie Moots was on hand looking rather slatternly with stringy hair and a shapeless dress. Lonzo was also there, moving erratically about and cackling in protest, "He's been sucking at a bottle and I want one, too — bound to be plenty of 'em, locked up behind the bar in that dining room — !"

Lassiter glanced about, saw several more of the pushing poles on deck, hardwood, pointed and metal-tipped at one end, with brass rings about the wood at intervals. He picked one up, plucked the lantern from Strunk, handed the pole to him. "Put your shoulders behind this!"

Strunk was scandalized. "I'm the master of this here vessel; I don't do that kind of work — !"

Gripping him by the scruff of the neck, Lassiter shoved hard;the red-nosed, ginger-whiskered man, overbalanced by his notable belly, all but went over the side. "Push!" Lassiter snapped. "And if there's any more drinking by you between here and LeGrande, I'll see to it you leak both blood and booze from a dozen holes in your hide!"

He handed the lantern to Effie. "Keep this light on the water, girl." Then he caught up another of the poles and took his place with the other three, probing with that metal tip for the underwater obstruction and finding it.

"When I count three," he said, "we shove, all together!"

He called the numbers, they thrust with straining effort, and the boat seemed to shudder sideways a little. "Again!" Lassiter snapped. "And still again and again, until we shake her free!"

It took half a dozen efforts before the boat slewed off the bar and was in the river's grip again.

All of them were gasping and blowing. Then Strunk yelped, "She'll broach to and capsize, nobody at that wheel!"

He went at a wobbling run to the stairway and up it to the texas. Lassiter meanwhile nodded to the two crewmen. "Good going," he said. "Now, keep up as full a head of steam as you can — and there'll be extra pay at LeGrande."

"Ha!" Effie exclaimed. "One more promise of cash that won't be kept!"

She confronted Lassiter in smoldering anger, "You had that high-toned, fancy woman in your room. I saw her, kiting out, her tail bare — !"

Lassiter gripped her frowsy dress, jerked her close. He said, gently but each word razor-edged, "Any more talk out of you, or any more cackles out of Lonzo, I'll stick the money due you between your teeth and throw both of you over the side!"

He flung her away. Once more she sat down hard — and her expression was indefinable as he stalked away.

Lassiter climbed the stairs also.

Stag Durkee spoke to him, drowsily, from a patch of shadow on the cabin deck, "I'm not behind you, *amigo* — just thought I'd let you know Lurie didn't rouse me, or I'd have been down there to lend a hand."

"Thanks. Next time around, if there is one, it might be plenty welcome," Lassiter growled. "Go finish your nap."

But then, as Stag started away, he added, "Wait! look, if you could use a stake, once we're at LeGrande — ?"

It had suddenly occurred to him that the man could be broke, or close to it, a condition with which Lassiter was not unfamiliar himself — and a Stag who was broke, eyesight dimming, head hurting, could be in for trouble.

"Well, thanks also . . . but I guess not. Too long a time of me staking others," Stag said, "and I don't think I could stand it, me having to take from somebody else. Maybe that Cananea deal — or something — will work out for me — "

Lassiter paced on. He paused outside Amy Follard's stateroom, but he shook his head. Not the right time or place now, he thought, and he went on to his own stateroom. A moment later he emerged again, bringing with him the third satchel, which he carried down to the main deck. There, making sure no one was watching, he shoved it under the tarp beneath the stairs.

Then he began a slow, steady round of the boat, aft on one side, forward on the other, as the best way to stay awake and last out the night.

He continued the pacing until first

light showed the canyon walls beginning to rise on either side, until a ruddy dawn brought the sun shining in a clear sky, the rain done.

Once again the boat hung itself on a sandbar, and more hard shoving was needed to free it. But after that the *Aurora* ran smoothly as hour succeeded hour. Lassiter found a spot on the main deck where he could watch everything. He settled down there, beginning to calculate ahead — arrival at LeGrande in the afternoon some time, and hopefully the whole deal might be wound up before dark.

He drowsed, trying to keep one eye open — but slipped finally into a stretch of deeper slumber, knowing he slept, testing with his senses and detected no reason for alarm.

Until, suddenly, he jolted awake, for a reason apparent to him before his eyes were fully open. The boat was quite still in the water again — but not in the stream, snagged and held again by a sandbar; instead, it was tied alongside a rickety stub of wharf, and only a glance was needed to recognize War Path Landing.

Lassiter sprang up. He saw Cap'n Strunk ashore, talking to a man there, alongside a high pile that, like the three satchels, was tarp-covered. Back aft on the shore side of the boat, the two crewmen were beginning to pitch aboard chunks from a stack of cut wood.

Long-striding, Lassiter leaped ashore. He went at Strunk, seized his arm. "You damned idiot, stopping like this!" he blazed.

"Huh? But I always stop here to load fuel, no place else for forty miles of river to do it," Strunk protested. And, "Hey, look at that — !" waving to the tarp-covered pile. "It's mining supplies, waiting on me for a haul up to Plumas. By Godfrey, I could make a tidy profit, coming right back, if I hadn't sold you the boat!"

He licked his lips, then. "How about a deal to buy it back? For some less, I hope, than you paid me — !"

Lassiter sent him at a headlong stagger toward the boat. "I'll give you the ratty hulk — but only if you cast off and get us out of here — !"

Stag Durkee's voice interrupted him, "*Peligro, amigo*! Danger . . . due in a couple of minutes, your head up for grabs just as sure as hell's hot — !"

Stag was on the cabin deck, pointing. Lassiter's head snapped around, and he saw them, riders in a column of twos, coming at a fast run from high ground eastward of the landing. No Milo Kershaw to lead them this time — it was Follard, himself, flourishing another pistol, after a fast pursuit through the night, Lassiter realized, and now they were attacking.

Muy peligroso, he admitted grimly. There were six of them, maybe, or even seven or eight. Stag's surmise Follard would recruit additional help was proving to be correct.

A glance showed the two crewmen scrambling aboard. Lassiter gripped his .44 and backed toward the boat. Bullets were already beginning to whine, guns barking yonder where Follard's bunch were hauling up, leaping down, coming on afoot.

Stag's gun roared, in response, but then Stag swore. "Can't see them clear," he called. "I'm backing you, *hermano*, but won't be any good until they're almost on top of me."

Lassiter leaped back aboard, looking about, feeling a rough rasp of frustration; he could make good use this instant of the bullets left in Effie's rifle, but it was in his stateroom. There was no axe in sight to cut the boat's lines again and no time to look for one.

But even as this thought crossed his mind, Lurie was running across the deck, leaping to the pier with a scissoring of legs — and she had an axe, swinging it at the forward line. Then, an instant following that, she was down, a limp heap, following the shrill howl of a ricochet.

Lassiter jumped ashore again and dropped to a knee beside her. Her features were still but no sign of blood showed on her face. Then he saw a red mark on her forehead, the skin shredded but not broken. A spent slug had creased her.

A fellow, maybe the one who had fired the bullet, was running at Lassiter with an obscene howl. He knocked him kicking at sixty feet. Then he cut that forward line with a swing of the axe, scooped up Lurie, and leaped back to the boat's main deck.

Stag, who had come down the stairway, shouted in fury and grief, lunging past Lassiter, who put the girl down. Stag was going at a couple of them, who, like fleeting shadows, had leaped aboard also, and were now firing at him. He hit one, the low body shot that characterized the expert gunhandler, then hit him again, and yet again before the man could fall, twisted and battered by the strike of each heavy slug.

"Save your bullets, *hombre*!" Lassiter advised sharply.

He chose the other one, also with

a solid body hit, but saw him come tenaciously on, trying with a slug of his own that missed. Lassiter had to spend another shell to drive him down — two of them dead lying close together, with a brutal splashing of blood, plus the one who had gone into the river, so Follard's bunch had been cut appreciably, maybe by half.

But Lassiter had a glimpse, from a corner of his eye, of two more shadowy figures leaping aboard the boat, somewhere aft. The *Aurora* was swinging broadside to the buffeting current, being rocked fiercely, but it was still held fast to the shore by the aft line.

Stag was kneeling beside Lurie, blunt fingers touching her cheeks. Lassiter spoke urgently, "She was only knocked cold. Cover me, Stag — !"

He headed aft, hearing above him some frantic yelling from Cap'n Strunk — and a shriek from Effie Moots.

He glanced up. She was on the stairway that rose above the three satchels, gripping her rifle, swinging it and firing, aiming aft. Someone came running from there, flushed out by her bullet, forced to attack. It was Suggs, the rawness of his face sharpened by hate and blood lust. Lassiter fired fast, steadily holding on him — but a violent lurch of the boat threw his bullet low, a leg hit for Suggs, who came on, spraying bullets wildly with the gun he held.

Lassiter killed him at about ten feet, then was eye-dazzled by a hot wink of light from a spinning wedge of steel, and only a very fast sideward jerk of his head saved him from a throwing hatchet, a throwback to the tomahawk wielded by Indian warriors.

The Indian who had thrown this one came bounding after it in a sinuous, twisting rush, now with a long, thin-bladed skinning knife in his fist, slashing wickedly with it.

Lassiter wasted one shot, trying to score another kill before he could get close, and then the one whom Amy had called Lame Wolf slammed into Lassiter. He was bare to the waist and greased, a wriggling, twisting instrument of destruction, but pitted against someone who had figured all the tricks of killing and had practiced the counter moves to balk them.

Not distracted by the knife, Lassiter did not let himself blunder into a counter move that would mean the two tugging and hauling at each other. Instead, he dropped his .44, caught Lame Wolf's left arm at the wrist and twisted him away, making use of the knife impossible for a second. Then he clamped the arm with his other hand and whipped it, then corkscrewed it, a move which forced Lame Wolf into a somersault, while he was flying at the railing.

He hit that with his back, just above the waist, and gave a thin cry. He hung for an instant, agony distorting his dark features, his back probably broken — at least, this had been Lassiter's cold intent — before he slid down, hitting the deck on his face.

But, like a rattler, he could still wriggle and fang. Lifting himself a little, he poised the knife to throw, hate wrenching his features.

With Lassiter cramped for space by the narrow deck, it was not so far-fetched an effort. However, bending, scooping up the .44, swinging it, firing, all in one swift blur of motion, he ended the capacity of lone Wolf to cause trouble. The Indian had miraculously escaped from the Kiskadee but there was no miracle escape for him this day.

Glancing up to Effie Moots, Lassiter lifted his hand. "Thanks!" he called, for the bullet which had driven Suggs to him. And, "Throw down your Henry to me. I need it, bad."

She had gone into his stateroom to retrieve the rifle, but she complied, while saying, "One more prowling the boat, I think, and one left ashore with that joker who has a face full of hair."

A crashing of gunfire came from the opposite side of the *Aurora.* Lassiter hurried around the cabin structure.

Stag, standing over Lurie's inert body,

was conducting a ferocious duel with somebody back along the starboard side of the boat. His gun abruptly snapped on an empty shell. He grimaced, features heavy, as though to say that this was the end of Stag Durkee.

But Lassiter, Henry stock against his shoulder, had sighted Stag's antagonist hugging a cabin wall aft. With one bullet he tagged him, then with another downed the man, who fell and, sliding as the boat rocked, wound up partially under the railing, head and one trailing arm almost in the river.

Stag spoke. "So damned much blood! Look!"

He pointed. Lassiter saw dark oily streaks on the river's gray-green surface. A lot of blood had spilled, all right; he could smell it, together with much burned powder. He said, "Stag, you out of lead?"

"Yeah. Nothing but lint in my pockets to throw if any more of them come at us," Stag replied. Then he settled down beside Lurie and took the girl in his arms as she stirred, with a thready sigh and a moan.

Lassiter caught up the axe, began to run with it. The line aft still held and its drag was still holding the boat sideways in the river's battering force. He leaped over the man he had just downed, ran on, with a sideward glance into the boat's engine room, the two crewmen pressing themselves into a corner there.

Suddenly, bullets were screaming again, all about him, ripping splinters, ricocheting from metal. He sent a harried look ashore, saw two of them — one was Jason Follard — by that pile of mine supplies, both firing fast, aiming at him.

Just as he realized this, he was hit, a dull, rough blow at the back of his neck; and he was down thinking, this is the end.

15

LASSITER sprawled on the deck of the rickety river boat, wits dulled, almost out. Both guns ashore crashed again, with a near whistling of bullets; the two survivors had him in plain sight and were trying to make sure of his finish by shooting him to rags. It stirred a sudden revivifying gust of anger.

Also, the pain at the back of his neck did not feel quite like a bullet strike. He twisted, discovered something was pressing down on him, realized it was a rather heavy scantling shaken loose by the boat's erratic motion.

With this, the fierce vitality which had carried him through so many crises surged like a geyser within Lassiter. He hauled himself up and went on, legs uncertain for several steps but then firming.

He was carrying both Effie's rifle and the axe, but he forebore from pulling trigger at that malignant pair ashore, concentrating with a single-minded intensity of purpose on the line that still bound the *Aurora* to the river bank. Stretched tight, it was thrumming with intense strain. It was a wonder it had not broken or pulled out the cleat around which it was wrapped on the boat's deck.

And a wonder as well, Lassiter thought, that he was managing to survive from second to second in the hail of bullets from Follard and his sole remaining follower — thanks possibly to the rage and hurry of Follard, both of these increasing as seconds passed with Lassiter still not hit.

Lassiter swung the axe, and once more the tough, tightly woven rope resisted the first bite of steel. He measured the swing of his arm, ignoring the whine and hiss of flying lead, and he swung again, with the blade now slicing deep — and a third time, and the rope parted, with a twanging sound, the line lashing like a striking snake.

He instantly relinquished the axe and caught up the rifle, holding it at aim but timing the first galvanic lurch of the freed boat. Yonder at the river bank, beyond a narrow but fast-widening strip of water, Follard was coming at a run — trailing the last member of his bunch, who was almost at the bank, pausing to slap hand against hip, to brace one of the long-barreled Colts so popular in the cavalry for three fast showy shots.

Lassiter, feeling no plunge of striking lead yet, still waited, not wanting to miss because of the river's action. Then, feeling the boat rising to a wave crest, holding there for an instant, he lined his sight on the other, aware of a broad stubbled face, of eyes suddenly alight with fear, of a convulsive swallowing as the man fired the pistol a fourth time, trying desperately for a bit.

At maybe eighty feet, Lassiter triggered a bullet into the bulk of his body, saw him jerk to the strike of the Henry's heavy chunk of metal and spin aside, falling. He was someone whose name he would likely never know, or give a damn about knowing, only another somebody who had bet his life on the skill and quickness of his hand to find it was second best.

Off beyond that downed body, Follard cried out, with a choked sound which spoke of intense rage. Lassiter tried to shift the rifle to cover him and to sight and fire again. But the boat was swinging; he could not hold steady, and when he did try a hurried shot, there was the sharp click of a hammer striking nothing, to warn of all bullets spent.

The boat was continuing to swing, as it headed downriver. Lassiter started back forward along the deck. Follard came into view again, now close to that pile of mine supplies. Lassiter lifted his .44, the range long now and a hit chancey. Still, he tried a shot, hurriedly adjusted, tried harder — and heard still one more click.

Like Stag, he was now out of bullets; those shoved into his pocket before heading north from Plumas were all gone. He made a mental note to check the guns dropped by those who had died on the boat.

He climbed the stairway to the cabin deck, then on up to the texas and the wheelhouse with a sense the boat was now running reasonably well. Amy was at the wheel, steering the craft.

Cap'n Strunk was huddled down in a corner, moaning, shattered glass on the floor, a wheelhouse window shot out, indicating at least one bullet had been aimed this way.

"With the boat behaving so violently, I felt somebody had better take over, and you were — busy," Amy said.

Glancing back, Lassiter saw the paddlewheels moving sluggishly. There was some steam to help in steering.

His gaze shifted to War Path Landing. Follard still stood by the stack of mine supplies, looking after them. And Amy said, "He'll keep coming after us, as long as he is alive . . . "

Perhaps, he thought, and told her, "You're doing fine. Just keep on steering. I'll spell you after a while."

Time began to pass, with the *Aurora* rushing down the wild river. The canyon walls were high on both sides for a while. White water boiled in churning froth at stretches of rapids, and it seemed a miracle the boat did not have its underside ripped out by some granite snag.

Lassiter checked about. Lurie was sentient again, wan and pale, steady on her feet — looking, in fact, steadier than Stag, who seemed to have been drained of energy. Perhaps he was suffering another headache. And maybe he was only thinking of LeGrande. It could be an end of the line for him, with little or no money in his pockets and his pride barring him from asking for help.

Effie and Lonzo Moots were together. Lassiter handed back her rifle. "Sorry I had to shoot it empty," he said.

"Hell, that don't matter," she replied,

in her profane manner, which seemed somehow less abrasive. "Listen, watching you knock over those jokers was something I won't ever forget!"

He studied her for a moment. She was a girl forced to grow up too soon and not yet quite a woman, who had in some measure made up for her earlier behavior: "Effie; I'll pay you and Lonzo what I promised, soon. We should be reaching LeGrande by about sundown."

Then he discovered something. Lonzo had gone about the boat, pushing overboard those who had died in the try to finish Lassiter — and he had also thrown their guns into the river.

"It seemed right," Lonzo said. "A man had ought to be buried with his weapons, like the Indians do it!"

Restraining with an effort an impulse to heave the simple-minded oldster into the river as well, Lassiter returned to the wheelhouse to relieve Amy, as promised.

Strunk was gone, thankfully — out of sight somewhere. Lassiter concentrated on the river, on every ripple, ridge, curl of foam which might warn of danger. It was suddenly afternoon, working along toward sunset.

After a while, he spoke to the woman, "Where do you want to go, once free of all this?"

"Home," she answered sighingly. "Where I spent most of my girlhood — Maryland. Just to live there for a while, for once not dependent on my mother's miserly relatives — !"

She would have company on her journey, then, Lassiter thought. Leaving Idaho, his next stop would be Washington . . . the Indian bureau.

More time passed. The canyon walls shallowed down, mostly gone. Then, Stag Durkee was suddenly at the wheelhouse door, looking in at him. "*Amigo*, you been keeping track of directions?"

"Yes. Due west for a good hour, now heading east again." Lassiter replied.

"We've been going around a long bend in the river — which means that scut, Follard, could cut straight across, for another swipe as we come along — and us without bullets," Stag said.

"Not much chance of getting at us, though, if we stay well out in the river," Lassiter said.

And this he meant to do. However, only moments later Amy suddenly cried out, pointing forward. He nodded tightly, had seen it also, a long riffle extending out from the bank on his right — a whole tree there, perhaps toppled and wedged. Lassiter spun the wheel. He kept spinning it, hopeful of somehow working around that menace, but the boat responded in a slow and turgid fashion.

The tree rammed the *Aurora*'s bottom with a long gouging rip.

Lassiter felt violent shivers run through the boat. He continued to spin the wheel, steering now toward the opposite side of the river where the bank was shallower. If they had to leave a sinking craft, he wanted a reasonable chance of making it ashore.

The *Aurora*'s bow ran up on a shallow shingle. It shuddered to a stop, then seemed to sigh wearily and quit.

Lassiter left the wheelhouse with Amy Follard. As they started down toward the main deck, he heard a yell and saw Cap'n Strunk leaving the boat, leaping with goat-like agility from deck to river bank, then turning to flip up a hand in a bitter, derisive gesture.

"Keep her; she's finished, and I'm bailing out," Strunk yelled. "For a high drunk in LeGrande tonight, since it's just around the next bend, only a couple of miles — !"

Watching him hustle away, Lassiter exhaled gently at this disclosure he had made it. But Amy's hand closed tightly on his arm. She breathed, in fright, "On that ridge — !"

It was a single rider, spurring fast toward the wrecked boat. However, peering intently, Lassiter murmured, "Ease up. He's a friend."

The rider was Anson Brett, springing down and striding fast toward the boat as Lassiter reached the main deck — Brett, facing him, hands clasped tightly together in strain. "Well — ? I've ridden this way along the river each of the past two days, knowing it was probably too soon, but — man, let me off the hook, fast!"

With the crook of a finger, Lassiter drew him to the tarp under the stairway, where he bent and pulled out two of the satchels. A moment after that Brett had one of them open, breathing hard as he saw its contents.

"By God! You did it!" he whispered.

"Delivery accomplished," Lassiter said. "I want fifteen hundred out of there, to pay an old man and a girl for helping me. Then you'll pay me twenty percent of the rest."

Brett fingered the blocks of bills. "I'm on fire with curiosity, of course, as to just how you did it — "

"Some other time, maybe," Lassiter said.

Down on one knee beside the opened satchel, Brett moistened his lips. "Tell me one thing, at least — about the whisper of additional money, from those Indian trading posts as they were closed, that cash perhaps shipped with Follard's detail — "

"You and I dickered only for return of the Army cash," Lassiter said.

"Then there *was* additional money! Look, I was ordered to soft-pedal talk about that — to rush it to the Indian Bureau in Washington, if recovered. But I can make a deal with them — "

"No dice, Brett," Lassiter said.

That money would be cut up enough as it was, Amy's share taken out; he was in no mood also to include Brett, especially not at this late date. Not that he was angry at Brett; Lassiter was always ready to grant any man the right to grab for what he thought he might take. And he continued, "I'll make my own deal, feel like a trip east anyway. Maybe I'll see you back there, Brett. If so, you're invited to dinner, champagne and lobster. However, as of right now — "

He pointed to the two satchels. "Make the payoff."

"Not here!" Brett protested.

"Here. Now," Lassiter said.

"Listen, there's something else we must talk about first, maybe another trip up the Kiskadee for you, but well worth your while; I've been authorized to offer a ten thousand dollar reward for whoever planned and carried out the theft of this money . . . dead or alive — !"

"No!" Lassiter said incisively.

Not that he had a particular objection to collecting on any reward; but he had had enough of Follard; he wanted the whole thing wound up before Follard showed again, and he said, "Start counting that cash — "

With no warning whatever, no startled cry, no shouted threat, an ear-splitting crack of sound seemed to tear the warm afternoon apart. The deck surged up hard under Lassiter's feet, hurling him with violence against a cabin wall. The whole boat was wrenched and twisted by the explosion.

Lassiter found himself sprawled on deck, head ringing, ears still numbed by that blast. He saw Brett on his back, eyes open but dazed. Both satchels had been hurled along the deck. Money had been spilled from the opened one, the wrappers broken, with a scattering drift of bills, some of them begining to blow as a hot breeze sprang up — and some of those fluttering over the side, to be whisked away by the river.

Lassiter realized what had happened, something whose possibility he should have foreseen. Follard had found that stack of mine supplies at War Path Landing. He had dipped into them, he had come fast across the narrow neck of land to intercept the boat here, he had acted — and, Lassiter felt beyond any doubt, would act again.

Beginning to haul himself up, he saw Amy appear, going at an unsteady pace to the tarp under the stairway. A smear of blood from a shallow cut showed on one cheek. She reached to take out the third satchel — she had known it was there, and now was acting on her own. The woman held the satchel for a moment, glancing toward him, then she pointed southward and went away, around to the forward part of the boat.

Lassiter started after her. He heard a cry like the hunting call of a hawk, and glanced back, to see Effie Moots, running about on deck, snatching up blowing bills — and Lurie as well, both stuffing their finds under the necklines of their dresses.

He kept going, rounded the cabin structure to see buckled, broken deck planking — picked his way across that, leaped to the shallow shingle of sand and run up the river bank, with a sense that never before in his life had there been a need to move more quickly or more surely.

Beyond the bank he saw a rising slope, heavily carpeted by brush, thick springy stuff almost head-high on a man. Half a dozen steps should take him to cover in it. With luck, even bare-handed, he might have a chance to fight from there, and he took three of those steps at sprinting speed.

Then the hope died as Jason Follard

snapped, "Damn you, freeze — or else start carrying your guts in your hands!"

Follard stood about thirty feet away; had come out of the brush around to Lassiter's right, a lighted cigar between his teeth, a .45 gripped in his fist. Covered by the gun, Lassiter stopped.

Follard shifted his attention — but with an eye still on Lassiter — to Amy, hurrying off southward along the bank. He shouted, "Stop right there, you conniving, thieving bitch . . . until I have time to deal with you!"

Amy looked around at him. Her pace faltered. As ordered, she stopped.

Follard glanced to Lassiter again, appraised his holstered .44, and seemed to grin mockingly behind his masking tangle of whiskers. "Out of shells — or just without the backbone to try for me?" he inquired.

Not waiting for a reply, he hurried on, "My dear wife, I notice, has one of the satchels. You have none. Therefore, I deduce the other two are still on that boat."

Then, glancing past him, at an angle of sight which included the *Aurora*'s port side, "Yes, I can see some clownish bastard who has them — he's running about, grabbing at some of the money which, has spilled out. Well, he shall surrender all of it, within a couple of minutes. After I have disposed of you — and I have a most satisfying plan for doing that."

Transferring the .45 to his left hand, Follard now dipped his right hand into a coat pocket and brought out something, an object like a short section of broomstick, wrapped in yellowish-red paper.

It was what he had brought along from those mine supplies.

Follard chuckled. "I like it this way, apt repayment for your use of the giant powder," he said. "But when I drop this stick at your feet, you won't be something like a burned log, as was the case with poor Kershaw. Instead, you will be nothing — dust, blown away by the wind."

Lassiter, who had done some work

with dynamite and knew its devastating power, quivered inwardly. The stick was fused with a short fuse; he had seconds only in which to act. But how? He could see no way out of this.

Eyes glittering, Follard lifted the stick to his cigar and fired it. He held the stick then. Sparks flew, flame eating swiftly toward the explosive; he obviously meant to wait until what he regarded as the last possible moment. It came; he threw the stick at Lassiter, in the same motion going sideways, toward the shelter of that brush.

Lassiter threw himself forward with a furious burst of speed and strength. He leaped very high, with a flick of his hand, all of the swiftness and surety he possessed in that gesture. He plucked the stick out of the air, and sent it flying back at Follard in a high lob.

For a breathless fraction of a second, before he hurled himself down and away, rolling fast, arms up to protect his face, hands over his ears, Lassiter saw Follard's mouth sag in horror, heard him begin to scream, while pulling the trigger of his .45, just once. Then there was the deafening crack of sound, the convulsive leap of earth, the battering shock wave.

After a long minute, Lassiter sat up. He slowly hauled himself erect, feeling shaken, wrenched — but unhurt.

Before him a pall of dust momentarily obscured the slope above the river bank. It began to blow away, showing the gouge of a crater and a few wisps of smoke.

Of Follard there was no trace whatever. He was the one who had been blown to dust, his vaunting dreams of glory ended forever.

Southward, Amy was looking this way as though still held by the strange mesmeric effect he had had on her. But now she stirred, began to back off, turned and walked away, at a quickening pace.

Lassiter headed toward the boat, as startled, inquiring cries came from there. Lurie had appeared with Stag, and now Effie and Lonzo Moots were showing also. Lassiter had to smile; both girls resembled pouter pigeons with cash stuffed under the tops of their dresses.

Then Anson Brett appeared also, lugging the two satchels of Army cash. He shouted wrathfully, "Stop them; they're thieves! So are a couple of black men who grabbed some of the money! Well, they're all going to give it back — !"

Lassiter gestured to the others to move out. "Brett, so what if a few thousand did — er — blow into the river, as a result of those dynamite blasts? Washington can't squawk much. Anyway, all they have to do is run the printing presses at the mint for a few minutes extra — "

He winked, as Brett stared at him, suddenly angry no longer — realizing, as Lassiter had hinted, that Washington must accept his count as to how much of the cash was left. And if Brett could seize the opportunity for a discreet lining of his own pockets, that would be strictly Brett's business.

Leaving, Stag Durkee said, "*Adios, amigo.* That gal sure turned my luck around! I've got me a real stake — might try Cananea again, might find myself a real silver mountain!"

Lurie nodded a good-bye, murmuring, "I hope we shall — will? — meet again soon."

Effie Moots said pertly, "Me and Lonzo are more than quits with you, mister. Come see us again sometime, but don't wait too long. I'm growing up awful Goddam fast!"

Lonzo cackled, like Cap'n Strunk no doubt planning an epic drunk.

Lassiter started to move also, with a final word, "Brett, I'll see you tonight for my pay-off. As for that reward you mentioned, forget it. There's nobody left to pay it on."

He lengthened his stride, to overtake Amy. But there was no need; she was coming back to him, hurrying.

"I was still a coward, starting to run one more time even when there was no need, for you had set me free," she said.

"But it won't ever happen again."

Lassiter took the third satchel, tucked it under his arm, put his other arm about her. "Not ever again," he agreed. "Now, we're in for a long trip, in style, east to Maryland. But first — LeGrande, tonight . . . "

A dimple showed briefly in her cheek, and excitement in her eyes. "Yes!" she said.

And about a month of high living ahead of them, before he left her for other men to court — before he was pulled back to far horizons, high peaks, vast stretches of lonely land where a man's strength was all that mattered.

It was the only life worth living, for Lassiter. He would be quite ready for it when danger and conflict beckoned again.

Right now, this choice woman beside him to help enjoy and spend what he had won, Lassiter was quite pleased with the way everything was going. He made a mental note, though, to stop at the first store they reached, in the town now beginning to appear ahead, to buy some bullets.

Plenty of bullets . . . just in case . . .

THE END

McALLISTER
ON THE
COMANCHE CROSSING
Matt Chisholm

The Comanche, McAllister owes them a life — and the trail is soaked with the blood of the men who had tried to outrun them before.

QUICK-TRIGGER COUNTRY
Clem Colt

Turkey Red hooked up with Curly Bill Graham's outlaw crew. But wholesale murder was out of Turk's line, so when range war flared he bucked the whole border gang alone . . .

CAMPAIGNING
Jim Miller

Ambushed on the Santa Fe trail, Sean Callahan is saved by two Indian strangers. But there'll be more lead and arrows flying before the band join Kit Carson against the Comanches.

GUNSLINGER'S RANGE
Jackson Cole

Three escaped convicts are out for revenge. They won't rest until they put a bullet through the head of the dirty snake who locked them behind bars.

RUSTLER'S TRAIL
Lee Floren

Jim Carlin knew he would have to stand up and fight because he had staked his claim right in the middle of Big Ike Outland's best grass.

THE TRUTH ABOUT SNAKE RIDGE
Marshall Grover

The troubleshooters came to San Cristobal to help the needy. For Larry and Stretch the turmoil began with a brawl and then an ambush.

WOLF DOG RANGE
Lee Floren

Will Ardery would stop at nothing, unless something stopped him first — like a bullet from Pete Manly's gun.

DEVIL'S DINERO
Marshall Grover

Plagued by remorse, a rich old reprobate hired the Texas Troubleshooters to deliver a fortune in greenbacks to each of his victims.

GUNS OF FURY
Ernest Haycox

Dane Starr, alias Dan Smith, wanted to close the door on his past and hang up his guns, but people wouldn't let him.

DONOVAN
Elmer Kelton

Donovan was supposed to be dead. Uncle Joe Vickers had fired off both barrels of a shotgun into the vicious outlaw's face as he was escaping from jail. Now Uncle Joe had been shot — in just the same way.

CODE OF THE GUN
Gordon D. Shirreffs

MacLean came riding home, with saddle tramp written all over him, but sewn in his shirt-lining was an Arizona Ranger's star.

GAMBLER'S GUN LUCK
Brett Austen

Gamblers seldom live long. Parker was a hell of a gambler. It was his life — or his death . . .

ORPHAN'S PREFERRED
Jim Miller

Sean Callahan answers the call of the Pony Express and fights Indians and outlaws to get the mail through.

DAY OF THE BUZZARD
T. V. Olsen

All Val Penmark cared about was getting the men who killed his wife.

THE MANHUNTER
Gordon D. Shirreffs

Lee Kershaw knew that every Rurale in the territory was on the lookout for him. But the offer of $5,000 in gold to find five small pieces of leather was too good to turn down.

RIFLES ON THE RANGE
Lee Floren

Doc Mike and the farmer stood there alone between Smith and Watson. There was this moment of stillness, and then the roar would start. And somebody would die . . .

HARTIGAN
Marshall Grover

Hartigan had come to Cornerstone to die. He chose the time and the place, and Main Street became a battlefield.

SUNDANCE: OVERKILL
John Benteen

When a wealthy banker's daughter was kidnapped by the Cheyenne, he offered Sundance $10,000 to rescue the girl.

RIDE A LONE TRAIL
Gordon D. Shirreffs

The valley was about to explode into open range war. All it needed was the fuse and Ken Macklin was it.

HARD MAN WITH A GUN
Charles N. Heckelmann

After Bob Keegan lost the girl he loved and the ranch he had sweated blood to build, he had nothing left but his guts and his guns but he figured that was enough.

SUNDANCE: IRON MEN
Peter McCurtin

Sundance, assigned to save the railroad from a murder spree, soon came to realise that he'd have to fight fire with fire, bullets with bullets and death with death!